WINTER'S DISSENSION

CONNOR WHITELEY

Copyright © 2020 CONNOR WHITELEY

All rights reserved.

ACKNOWLEDGMENTS
Thank you to all my wonderful readers without you I couldn't do what I love.

CHAPTER 1

The Fire crackled.

Roaring to life.

Alvis smiled as he breathed in the heavenly aromas of the fresh cooking meat on the large open fire with a massive ring of smooth black stone around the edges.

Preventing the children playing nearby from getting to close to the fire.

The embers burned bright red.

Sizzling meat filled the air.

Alvis continued beaming his delight. His oldish face of about 60 years wrinkling as his smile grew and grew.

Turning his head, Alvis saw the beautiful, stunning, life filled market.

All around him, thousands of Insenguardians were chatting, laughing and buying their daily goods.

Tens of bakers, sewers, forger and tens of other professions all gathered in this beating heart of Insenguard. Standing behind their large rectangular oak table laid out their goods.

Alvis old heart skipped a few heartbeats looking at everyone.

All the Insenguardians in their long silky blue, red, yellow or black dresses or causal wear were all cramped around tables chatting about god knows what with each other and the stall owners.

Golden coins and goods changed hands.

Children cheered in utter delight at their new toy or sweet treat.

This is why Alvis loved Insenguard.

It was a country of love, community and hope.

This was a place for everyone to be able and thrive.

Alvis stepped forward towards a stall in front of him.

He felt the fresh smooth cobblestone beneath his feet.

Although, the only thing that puzzled Alvis about

his new country was that the market was organised by a grid of cobblestoned paths for people to walk on.

Yet the stalls were on the fresh bright green grass.

What happened if it rained?

Would the market stalls sink?

The smell of the fresh meat behind Alvis caught his attention.

He needed to get some of that succulent fresh buffeater meat.

Alvis paused.

Trying to remember what a Buffeater was.

His face lit up amazed he remembered what a Buffeater was.

It was a large rodent the size of a wolf or Werecat.

Alvis shivered as he despised the look of the oversized rats but he had to admit between two slices of spiced bread. They were damn well delicious.

Turning his attention to the stall in front of him, Alvis gave an involuntary gasp of awe as he looked at all the beautiful suits, shirts and watches on the oak stall in front of him.

Popping up his head, he saw a young stunning woman with thick blond hair behind the stall. Wearing a silky well-fitting dress.

She stared at him in surprise and she looked as if she was going to either kneel before him or run away.

In a petite, smooth voice, the girl managed: "Chancellor,"

She nodded her head slightly in respect.

Alvis paused for a moment.

His eyes widened as he realised what she meant.

In a posh, composed, well-spoken voice, he replied: "I apologise, Daughter of Insenguard, I am still getting used to that title. It was only last night when the Empress made me Chancellor,"

Clearly, the woman was still in shock at talking to someone who had been in the Empress' presence.

"Um, of course, my Lord. Why do you come down here with us mortals?"

Alvis gave a loud chuckle.

"Daughter, you must remember we are all the same in the eyes of the Empress, and my friend, you come from Gauic I presume judging by your accent,"

The woman sank a little.

"Um yes, my Lord and you?"

"Northern Gauic. It has been a chaotic week, hasn't it?"

The woman gave a friendly smile.

Alvis was partly relieved to have another one of his kin in Insenguard. At least someone else had survived.

The torturous memories of whipping, Slaughter, blood and burning cities filled his mind.

The woman placed a hand on his arm.

She withdrew it immediately.

"I'm so sorry, my Lord. I shouldn't be touching or walking the same air as..."

Alvis waved her silent.

He turned slightly and gestured with his hand to the beauty of the market and surrounding city of Insenguard.

"Nobody would have thought just a week ago that the Empress and her forces had reconquered their homeland. Not a single mark of those dark times. Yet Insenguard only had a small military after their Conquest. So, they had no citizens,"

The woman gave a friendly smile.

"No, my Lord. As soon as I heard they conquered Insenguard. I packed up my family and fled. The madness, war and burning of Gauic. And you, my Lord? I know you were in the North. That's semi-independent, right?"

Alvis paused.

Gathering up the courage to retell his short tale.

He let out a long deep breath.

A tear welled up in his right eye.

"Yes, Daughter of the Empress, but the North had it worse. My wife was tortured, her limps ripped from her body. My unborn son was chomped out of her womb by the wolves. My infant son was thrown off a cliff by the Gauic King. My wife screamed for me to find and continue to do good. You see I was the Chancellor for the King as well. But I disagreed with him. But when news reached me of Insenguard being free. I joined the masses in travelling here,"

Alvis smiled. Feeling a heavy load off his chest.

The woman nodded.

Looking around the market.

"That's why we're all here Chancellor. The Empress offered us hope and a new life. That's why I will die for her before I see Insenguard fall,"

Alvis quickly nodded.

Turned away to wipe his eyes and turned back to her.

"My friend, I am attending the Funeral followed by the Empress' Departure Feast tonight. Could I buy a black Insenguardian Suit please?"

The woman almost ignored him.

Picking out a stunning long black tight suit with wondrous gold threads running throughout the fabric.

Alvis gave her some coins including a very healthy tip, nodded his thanks and took the suit.

Without thinking, he dashed over to the fire and bought himself some of the freshly cooked meat.

The fresh delicious meat filled his nose and senses.

Holding up the brown bread bun filled with the freshly cooked meat, Alvis chomped down on it.

His mouth exploded with the fresh earthy flavours of the spices.

He beamed with delight.

"Go away!" the woman screamed from the clothing market stall.

Alvis shot around.

He saw two large men standing at her stall.

Two pistols drawn.

Their long black cloaks blowing in the light warm wind.

Everyone slowly backed away.

Alvis walked over to the men.

The taller of the brutish men turned to face Alvis.

Whipping out his badge of authority.

He was an Officer of Justice.

Alvis rolled his eyes.

Becoming very annoyed that he wasn't able to finish enjoying his meat sandwich.

"What is the issue, Officers?" Alvis calmly spoke.

"Go away, Chancellor. This is none of your business,"

"What is the issue please?"

"Go away, Chancellor! I mean it. You have no authority outside a council meeting. You are nothing but a glorified chairman!"

Alvis laughed hard.

"What is the…" Alvis started.

The smaller of the brutes answered: "She is a Gauic, a scum,"

Alvis' hands formed fists.

Before he dropped them.

Gesturing to the surrounding markets, Alvis added: "No, she is not Gauic. She may have been there, but she is an Insenguardian. As are we all Officers. We have all fled nightmares and torture. We are all Insenguardians now,"

The Officers pointed their weapons firmly at the woman.

The Chancellor walked over to them.

Standing in front of the guns.

He chuckled.

"By the Power invested in me by the God Empress, I declare you drop your weapons, and you leave this woman alone. She is now under the Direct Protection of the Throne under the Refugee Act subsection 8c,"

The Officers looked at one another, unsure.

"Do not throw your lives away by committing a Capital Offence,"

The Officers lowered their weapons and ran away.

Alvis turned to her.

"Oh, thank you, my Lord. Is that Act even real?"

"Heavens no, my dear. I made it up. He was right. I have no power outside of Council Meetings. Now, my dear, I must go back to my sandwich,"

CHAPTER 2

Glaring towards the massive black steel stage, Alvis watched the Empress give her honourable noble words of righteousness to the masses.

Alvis stood against the immense stone walls of the fortress on the left-hand side of the equally immense chamber.

Alvis had to admire the craftsmanship of the chamber. It was easily the size of ten football pitches and ten stories high with immense cold blocks of grey stone.

Running his fingers across a stone block, Alvis gave a slightly inappropriate laugh as the odd rough texture of the stone tickled him.

A few nearby soldiers looked at him, frowning.

Turning his head to the right, sweat slowly formed on his forehead as he saw tens of thousands of soldiers in their thick black and gold Knight armour.

The thought of being in a room with so many Insenguardian soldiers made Alvis drink his tall slim glass of Insenguardian champagne a bit quicker.

A part of Alvis wanted to leave as his stomach kept churning.

He felt like an outsider.

He was one.

How could Alvis ever hope to fit in with these 'true' Insenguardians?

Turning his head back to the Empress, Alvis had to admit she was a beautiful woman and that voice.

Despite, Alvis being tens of metres away from the stage, which was tens metres of tall itself, Alvis appreciated her speaking skills.

A part of him smile at that bit, he hated public speaking.

Occasionally, he had to address his former nation but he always sweated through his clothes.

Apparently, he was good at it, but he still despised public speaking.

This just made Alvis love his new home even more.

A round of appals erupted as the Empress bowed.

Everyone in the chamber clapped as loudly as they could to show their devotion and love for the Empress' kind and truthful words about their fallen friends and family members.

The Empress waved her hand.

Everyone stopped.

A gentle hummed filled the chamber.

Alvis looked puzzled.

All the soldiers moved towards the edges of the chamber.

The floor rumbled.

Alvis rose on his toes to try and see.

He barely managed to see.

He saw the floor open.

A pyre of dead chopped up corpses appeared.

He looked at the Empress.

Her eyes met his.

In a smooth authoritative voice, she proclaimed: "per Insenguardian Funeral traditions, now we burn the bodies of our victorious dead. So, please stay and talk, watch your friends burn and most importantly celebrate their lives,"

Alvis nodded his thanks at the explanation.

With a flick of her hand, the ten pyres became engulfed in golden dancing flames.

The soldiers moved forward.

Standing in small groups around each pyre.

Talking, celebrating their fallen friends as they watched their friends burn to Ash.

Alvis slowly walked towards the burning pyre in front of him.

He squeezed past a few soldiers, who sneered at him for gliding past.

Alvis ignored them.

He walked towards the flames.

They crackled loudly as the bodies burned.

The Chancellor flinched expecting the flames to be too hot.

Yet they were not.

The flames danced brightly with magical passion.

Licking the bodies clear of flesh, muscle, and bone.

For Insenguard knew the truth of reality, in the end, we are all ashes to ashes.

Silence fell across the chamber.

No one talked.

Even the flames fell silent.

Alvis turned around.

Everyone was looking to a large iron door a few metres from him.

Immense golden armoured warriors marched out.

Soldiers were quickly parted.

Creating a path towards Alvis.

Everyone but Alvis sank to their knees.

More golden warriors poured out.

Creating a perfect barrier from the masses of soldiers to prevent them from getting anywhere near the Chancellor.

Alvis looked at the doorway.

He dropped to his old knees.

The cold floor paining him.

The Empress of Insenguard walked carefully

towards him.

"Rise," she commanded.

Alvis couldn't.

Not because of his old or ancient bones.

He couldn't because he was in sheer awe of being in the presence of a divine being like the Empress.

Whilst he had spoken to the Empress before. He still couldn't resist the immense aura of power, warmth and awe she created.

Staring at the Empress, Alvis noted her stunning golden dress with her long thick brown hair as well as her youthful features.

"Rise," she commanded.

Alvis complied.

Forcing himself up.

Still in awe at her almighty presence.

Looking at the soldiers behind the Guards' barrier, Alvis witnessed their confusion and if was almost like they were trying to see something that wasn't there.

"Relax, Chancellor. Using my magic, I have created a shroud shield around us. To them, we are mere shadows. I could kill you and they would merely see two figures standing here,"

A massive two-metre golden warrior covered with jewels and wearing a thick red cloak marched up behind the Empress.

He smashed his immense golden Bladed Staff onto the stone floor.

Cracking it.

His eyes narrow and determined.

Alvis sank a little.

The Empress smiled, waving a hand to relax the guard.

"Alvis, please relax. You are the last person I want to kill,"

The Chancellor rose a little.

"Of course, my Lord Empress. May I inquire to why you want to meet with me in such a fashion? The shroud, I mean, my Lord,"

"Abbie, please. I have news for you Alvis. I am leaving Insenguard tomorrow to travel to the Global Security Headquarters half a world away. I have completed all the essential and non-essential tasks to reforge Insenguard,"

Alvis' eyes narrowed.

Taken in shock by the news.

"My Lady, it has been a week. Is Insenguard ready for you to leave, my Lord?"

"Alvis, I have extremely effective systems in place. I have already dispatched my Children and the Death Cult on their missions. I have to do my part for the Homeland as well. Anyway,"

Empress Abbie clicked her fingers.

The immense golden warrior next to the Empress passed her a file.

Alvis's eyes were wild with each move of the immense golden warrior.

The Empress laughed.

"Do not mind, my Praetorian, Chancellor. He is thankfully devoted to his work of protecting me. Take this," she passed him the file.

Alvis took the file with shaky hands.

Excepting the Praetorian to kill him for getting within striking distance of his Empress.

He got the file and started to read it.

"The file details your new Council of Insenguard. More of your responsibilities are detailed in the file, but in short you are the Chairman. It is your job to ensure things run smoothly. Any trouble contact me personally. I wish you the best of luck," she explained to him.

The Empress turned away.

"Lord Chancellor," she nodded her goodbye.

"Lord Empress," he bowed.

The Empress and her praetorian guard started to march away.

Alvis flicked through the file.

The damp paper feeling weird in his fingers.

He knew some of the names.

Wait, there was one name he DID recognise.

"My Lady?" he asked.

The Empress kept walking.

The Chancellor walked towards her.

He passed two Guards.

He was thrown to the floor.

His face smashed into the floor.

His arms pulled behind him.

He screamed.

A massive hand grabbed his throat.

It squeezed.

"Wait!" the Empress commanded.

The Guard stopped squeezing.

The Empress waved him to release the Chancellor.

He collapsed to the ground gasping for air.

The Empress bent down in front of him.

The Praetorian marched towards her.

Abbie waved a hand.

The Praetorian stopped.

"My Lady, why is Akuma on the Council of Insenguard? Isn't he the extremist from the Covert Military Division who wanted Insenguard to burn the world down and rebuild it in your Father's image?"

The Empress frowned.

Remembering the stupid sect of Insenguardians under her Father who actually believed that his intention with that off-the-cuff comment.

After a moment, her face relaxed.

She smiled.

"Yes, Alvis. You are correct. Have fun dealing with him,"

She kissed him on the cheek and walked away.

CHAPTER 3

Signing yet another document, Alvis picked up his blue cold mug if Insenguardian coffee and placed it firmly on his desk.

As the mug hit the desk, a tiny bit of the almost black coffee kicked into the air.

Filling Alvis' senses with woody and extremely bitter notes of the coffee grounds.

The Chancellor almost laughed at himself because back in Gauic he hated coffee. Yet in Insenguard he couldn't get enough of it.

How times change, he thought.

Pushing himself away from his desk for a moment, he stood up.

Pacing around the small wooden office.

Stretching his ageing joints.

As he paced, Alvis admired the dark brown oak panels of the walls.

Part of him wondered how thick each panel must have been.

Yet the other part of him wondered how many more damn requisition forms he needed to read and sign.

When Alvis decided to accept the Empress' offer of becoming Chancellor he excepted to be a chairman of the Council.

Not have to sign permission forms for stupid expenses. Like, 5 years' worth of ink for the Emissary of the Foreign Office.

He wanted to change things, not sign for things.

Anyway, Alvis took a deep breath. Trying to breathe in more of the bitter coffee, to no prevail, and remembered his duty to the Empress.

He looked at his desk.

Admiring the spectrum of swirling, twirling patterns in the oak work with its immense 3 metre long panels and its four thick knobby legs.

Alvis admired the woodwork.

A slight tear swelled up in his eyes as he remembered his son had wanted to be a carpenter, and for a child, he was adept at woodwork.

But that was a dead life to Alvis.

It was time to start anew.

Then it hit the Chancellor how much more paperwork he needed to do as he witnessed the endless piles of files and documents almost growing out from his desk. Growing towards the ceiling.

Alvis placed his hands on one pile.

The cold morning air giving the paper a minor chill.

After flicking through some papers of the pile, he found the large thick folder the Empress had given him last night.

Even the thought of himself having to talk to Akuma later on irritated him.

His fingers twitched at the thought.

Although, Alvis gave a devilish smile as he thought of himself walking into the Council chamber and having absolute authority over these people in charge of various aspects of Insenguard.

Alvis pulled his thick well-holstered oak chair under him, a sharp edge of the nail digging into his back, and opened the file.

A small yellow note fell out.

The Chancellor bent down.

Thrusting the edge into his back.

He bit down on his lip.

Grabbing the note, Alvis straightened his back and read it.

His eyebrows narrowed.

It was something about the Empress giving him an Aide.

Alvis looked up in confusion.

He stood up.

Walked over to the large wooden circular door to his office.

Opened it.

Checked the long smooth wooden corridor.

To see nobody was there.

Alvis walked back over to his chair and sat down.

He retraced his steps.

He got to the office at 6 am, 3 hours before his start time, he left for ten minutes around 7 am for another coffee and he hadn't left since.

Alvis checked his plain copper pocket watch.

It was now 11 am.

The Chancellor laughed at himself for not noticing the time going by.

A knock pounded on the door.

Alvis rolled his eyes.

Sitting down, he commanded: "Come in,"

The massive circular door creaked open.

Scratching across the wooden floor.

Alvis looked up.

Biting his tongue.

He needed to find who was in charge of maintenance and get that fixed.

As a tall woman walked into the office, Alvis' eyes narrowed.

It was the woman from the market stall.

In partial shock, the Chancellor studied the woman.

Was she lost?

She wore a long silky blue dress that showed her defined slim body well.

In addition, her long thick blond hair was wrapped up in a ponytail.

Her youthful features and her well-defined jawline smiled at the Chancellor.

"Fair Daughter of Insenguard, may I inquire to what you're doing here?"

"Um, my Lord. I am your new Aide. Didn't the Empress tell you? She found me late last night,"

Alvis cocked his head.

"No, my dear. The Empress did not inform me, but I am glad you are here. It is good to see such a friendly face such as yours is,"

The woman gave a mocking bow.

"Fair Daughter of Insenguard, two things if I may. Why are you late? We start at 9 am and what is your divine Empress given name?"

The woman took a step back.

Her eyes wide.

Alvis gave her a friendly smile.

He was familiar with the custom that when some refugees had come to Insenguard. They had shredded their old names and the Empress gave them new ones.

"Um, my Lord. How did you know? I haven't told everyone that I spoke to the God Empress,"

Alvis ignored her.

Everyone had a story to Alvis.

In time, he would know hers but until then he was ready to be respectful.

"Aquene is my name. I was late because the Empress gave me permission to sell the last of my clothing. Now, I am completely dedicated to my God-given task,"

"I am Alvis. We are going to be working together so let us speak in first names when together and alone,"

"Of course, my… Alvis,"

The Chancellor stood.

Stretching his back.

"Aquene get my robes of Office, please. I want to get to the meeting Chamber before 12 to prepare,"

Aquene paused.

"What is wrong, my dear?" Alvis mentioned as he started to unbutton his blue silk jacket.

"Um, um, my Lord. There is no meeting,"

Alvis stopped.

Walked over to her.

His eyes narrow.

"Please Aquene, tell me what you mean?"

Aquene smiled a little at the awareness of the situation.

Alvis breathed deeply out of frustration.

Breathing in Aquene's flowery perfume.

"Per Insenguardian Law, a meeting between the council can only happen if all 8 members are present. Per my job description, I went to check with all the members before coming here. One member declined the meeting,"

Alvis gave a positive smile.

Inside, his blood boiled.

There was so much to discuss today.

There was urgent business needed to be dealt with.

"Alvis, you do have emergency powers to force a meeting to occur. But I doubt you meet the legal requirements for such an enactment of authority,"

The Chancellor backed away.

His hand on his forehead.

He nodded.

"Yes, yes, yes. I need a more dire situation to enact it without fear of repercussions from the Empress if someone reported me,"

Aquene frowned.

"Did this member give a reason for the Declined Meeting?"

Aquene smiled a little.

"Well, Alvis. That's where things get interesting. The Member of the Council didn't actually meet with me. I went to their office, but a Guard was waiting outside for me. It was the Guard who delivered the news to me,"

"So, the Member didn't even follow the protocols?"

Aquene shook her head.

Alvis placed his hands over his mouth thinking.

"Alvis, I can't tell you the Member for legal reasons, but I can tell you the Guard's armour colour,"

The Chancellor shot up.

His back straight.

"Of course, Aquene. I do not desire for you to get in trouble. But just out of curiosity, what was the Guard's armour colour,"

"Dark blue, my Lord,"

"Get my coat, Aquene. We need to have a firm chat with the Emissary,"

CHAPTER 4

After demanding the guards outside to let Alvis and Aquene into the Emissary's office to see her.

They both walked into the massive grandiose office.

No one was there.

Looking around the Chancellor felt belittled by the majesty of the office.

For its massive ten metre high walls were decorated in finely detailed gold carvings.

With grand depictions of battles in Insenguard's long history.

Alvis turned to Aquene.

He rolled his eyes.

Seeing her completely dazzled by the beauty of

the office.

Even the ceiling was a complete masterpiece as hundreds of tiny white golden angels had been painted by hand.

Alvis almost busted out laughing as he saw the final piece of the ceiling.

To top off the grandeur of the office was an immense solid gold chandelier with rubies and diamonds.

Alvis heard footsteps.

Both Alvis and Aquene turned their heads to the left to see a large reinforced wooden door.

It was shut firmly.

Yet the footsteps thundered towards them on the other side of the door.

Despite, the warm air in the Office. Alvis still felt like a blanket of cold darkness was descending over him.

He gestured for Aquene to take a seat.

She didn't want to.

Alvis walked over to the large, polished marble desk in front of them.

He ran his long bony fingers across the smooth

grey marble with golden veins running through it.

The rounded edges were freezing cold as Alvis' fingers reached them.

He shot his hand back.

Pulling out an immensely heavy throne-like chair made from pure granite. He sat down.

Resting his feet, cladded in fresh new black leather boots on the desk.

Aquene rushed over.

The Chancellor put up a hand to relax her.

Glaring at the desk, he was surprised that the desk was clean. It only had three piles of documents in the far corner nearest to Alvis.

Allowing any guest to admire the mighty skill it would have taken to carve such a gloriously smooth and heavy marble desk.

If Aquene wasn't with him, Alvis probably would have busted out in laughter at the ridiculousness of the Office.

This was the definition of overstatements and unadulterated aggrandizement.

Although, Alvis admired the Sectary of State's and the Empress' intentions of this Office.

The sole purpose of this Office was to intimate foreign guests and make them understand the power and wealthy of Insenguard.

"Dear Aquene, please sit down. Put your feet up,"

"My Lord, you can't put your feet up in another person's office. It's not right,"

"My dear Daughter of Insenguard, I am the Chancellor, and I am here on Council matters. There is no higher authority save the Empress on such matters,"

Aquene slowly complied.

She tentatively walked over to the large granite chairs and sat down.

Alvis beamed.

Knowing he was being extremely disrespectful.

The wooden door to their left scratched across the floor as it opened.

Alvis needed to find that maintenance person.

The Office was filled with the smell of burning fruit and sweets.

Aquene turned around to see the Emissary.

Alvis did not.

He focused on the desk.

He could feel Aquene sinking into herself as the Emissary pounded the floor as she walked towards them.

Her pounding feet echoed around the Office.

She pulled out her own golden granite chair and sat behind the desk.

Her eyes narrow at Alvis.

Smiling at the Emissary, the Chancellor noted her slim yet muscular figure in her tight dark blue dress.

Her short black hair was fanned out across her back.

Alvis met her glare.

The Emissary's youthful features were scarred slightly by war, but her eyes spoke of extreme determination and rage.

Now, he had her complete attention. Alvis removed his feet from her desk.

In a soft, velvety voice the Emissary spoke: "My Lord Chancellor, I take it you are not informed that it is a criminal offence to come here to discuss why I declined the meeting,"

Alvis simply smiled at her.

"My Lord Chancellor, you clearly forget where you are. Look around you. I am powerful. You do not want to make an enemy of me,"

Aquene breathed deeply.

Alvis waved her to relax.

"Emissary, fair and beautiful Emissary of Insenguard. I do not come here to seek trouble. I only want answers," Alvis said.

"As do I!" a loud thunderous voice boomed from behind them.

Alvis spun around.

His breathing quickened.

His heart raced.

Sweat dripped down his back.

Coating the back of the chair.

The Empress' Praetorian marched towards them.

His golden armour smashed into the floor as he walked.

His immense golden Bladed Staff chipped away at the marble floor.

The Praetorian stomped his feet in front of Alvis.

His cold black eyes fixed on the Emissary.

The Chancellor could smell his sweat and his manly senses.

Clearly, the Praetorian focused on duty over perfect personal hygiene.

Alvis looked at the hardened war scared face of the Praetorian.

The Chancellor felt vast uneasy hold take in his stomach as he thought about what this Praetorian was capable of.

"Praetorian, you can't come in here. You are the protector of the Empress nothing more," The Emissary demanded, pointing to the door.

"I am the Empress' Praetorian. Her safety is my only concern. She left me in Insenguard to watch all Her Realm. That is what I intend to do,"

"Ridiculous, Praetorian. You are nothing except a bodyguard. You're only concerned is Her protection. Isn't it true that you would let Insenguard burn and millions die as long as She is safe?" the Emissary shot back.

The Praetorian nodded.

"My sole focus is Her safety. That is what I am doing here. Why did you decline the Meeting? This jeopardised Insenguard's security and that IS a threat to the Empress,"

The Emissary released a deep breath.

Filling the air with fruity smells.

Alvis checked his watch.

He shook his head, a bit late for lunch but he had more important things to consider.

"Aquene," the Chancellor said, waving her to get off the chair.

She jumped up.

The Praetorian firmly sat down.

His fingers tight on his Bladed Staff.

The Emissary leaned over the desk slightly.

In a hushed tone, the Emissary spoke "My Lords, I declined a meeting because I believe there are… traitors on the Council, and I do NOT want them to influence events in Insenguard. Until these traitors are found I am refusing to call a Meeting,"

Alvis leaned back in his chair.

His mouth opened slightly.

He raised his hand to his forehead.

Rubbing it slightly.

The Praetorian stood up.

Alvis jumped.

Aquene took a few steps back.

The Chancellor wished he could do the same.

"That is a serious allegation, Emissary. The Empress personally appointed each of the Members of the Council. This is a serious threat to Her safety. What evidence do you have for these allegations?" the Praetorian boomed.

Alvis' eyes narrowed.

Slowly, the Emissary spoke: "Praetorian, whilst I despise you and your organisation. I will admit it is good you are here. A handful of the Members come from countries that have never been pro-Insenguard. I believe they would be traitors,"

Alvis laughed at her.

"Fair Emissary, this is not the time for racism or harshness. They are all Insenguardians now. I am from Gauic originally. They hated Insenguard. Now, I am a loyal Insenguardian. Do you have anything more concrete?"

The Emissary rolled her eyes and threw the Chancellor a thick file.

"Civil Unrest, my Lords. It is thriving since the Empress left late last night. Today, there is a massive crowd forming in the north of Insenguard. People are shouting, fighting and more. This is not the Insenguardian way,"

Alvis nodded as he looked at the reports.

The Praetorian spoke up, "What are the Lord Justice and the People's Representative doing?"

The Emissary knew she was in control.

She put her feet up on the desk.

Alvis read from the file an eyewitness report.

"It's my holy observation... the Lord Justice has failed to send any Officers to the crowd. Even after repeated requests were sent... oh, the People Representative refuses to comment or even attend the Crowd to calm down tensions,"

Standing up from her desk, the Emissary started to walk away. Before, the massive circular door shut behind her, she said:

"That should hopefully be enough for your curiosity. Now, I have to prepare for a meeting for with the Ambassador from Gauic. Be three grown-ups and show yourself out,"

She slammed the door behind her.

Aquene rolled her eyes.

The Praetorian started to walk out.

"My Lord Praetorian," Alvis demanded with authority.

The Praetorian stopped.

"This is a threat to the Empress. I agree. But may I suggest in Her interest, we team up. I will investigate the political angles and you investigate the Civil unrest. After all, you are a man of action, I am a weak politician,"

The Praetorian smiled.

"Flattery will not work with me, Chancellor. Yet I know the Empress choose you personally and with great pride. I will extend to you the smallest amount of trust I can afford. You investigate the Lord Justice and People's Representative,"

"Of course, and thank you, mighty Praetorian,"

Alvis and Aquene were about to walk out the door when the Praetorian added.

"But know this Chancellor, my concern is Her, not anyone else. If you walk down this path, do not rely on my protection. It will not come,"

CHAPTER 5

Ridiculous is all the Praetorian could use to describe what was happening.

Standing high above, the ant-like mortals of Insenguard, the Praetorian watched the crowd intensively.

Just waiting for the excuse to strike.

The high stone buildings around the square towered like giants over the crowd, with their multistorey.

In addition, the white cobblestone was completely covered by the thousands of people there.

All different heights, weights and body types.

Wearing everything you can imagine from the great silky dresses of business people to the white tunics of everyone else.

The Praetorian frowned.

There was no pattern here.

There should be some sort of pattern to this crowd.

In Insenguard, there was no nobility, no class, nor politics.

Well, unless you're inside the Council.

Again, the Praetorian frowned at the stupidity of the Council.

As far as he was concerned, all the other Council members were idiots.

In all honesty, the Praetorian would act and make the council do their duties to the Empress.

However, that could lead to the worse fate imaginable. The negligence of his duty to protecting the Empress.

He would never allow that.

Turning his attention back to the crowd below, he took a step closer to the edge of the roof.

The tiles moved and pressed their smooth rocky surface into his armoured feet.

The hot late afternoon sun beat down upon him.

Inside his ornate golden armour, the Praetorian felt a little amount of sweat run down his back.

He didn't care.

Looking down at the crowd, he saw the mass of people start to get excited as the large wooden stage in the centre of the stage was used.

A tall, elegant woman in a long purple cloak walked onto the stage followed by two brutal well-muscled bodyguards.

The Praetorian's training kicked in.

The bodyguards were young, male, non-Insenguardians origins.

The woman- Insenguardian military, fraction unknown.

If the Praetorian was capable of wrath or rage. Then he was sure that he would descend into a murderous rage at the thought of an Insenguardian solider could be involved.

When the woman got to the centre of the stage, she waved like royalty to the other citizens.

The Praetorian focused.

He quickly checked the other rooftops.

A mere mortal would have looked at the rooftop

and saw nothing.

Yet the Praetorian barely managed to make out the golden warrior of his other Guard members.

They had the square surrounded.

All they needed was a command from the Praetorian.

He snapped his attention to the stage as the woman began to speak in a demanding yet charming voice.

"Thank you, wonderful Insenguardians for coming today. Today I have requested your assistance and you have answered. Thank you. Now, us chosen can enact the Will of the God Empress,"

The Praetorian frowned with rage.

How dare this false prophet preach the false words of the Empress.

His Bladed Staff twitched for blood.

+My Lord, we cannot allow this to continue+ a fellow Guard echoed into the Praetorian's mind using the Empress' hive mind connection.

+Wait!+ he commanded.

"When we leave here, I urge all of you to take up arms and attack the unclean immigrants!"

The Praetorian laughed inside his armour.

This woman might have descended from the Insenguardian military. But that was a long time ago.

This was never the Insenguardian way.

Unlike other countries, the Empress had always understood the need for refugees and their value in society.

The woman continued: "Now, go out my glorious children and let us do the God Empress' Will!"

+NOW!+ the Praetorian barked.

All the Praetorian Guard jumped from the rooftops.

People screamed.

The Praetorian swung his Bladed Staff.

Blood spattered up the stone walls.

His fellow Guards secured the exits.

No one was going to leave.

The Praetorian charged forwards.

Men, woman, children screamed in terror at the Praetorian.

He pushed them aside.

A mass of people charged him.

Punching him.

Kicking him.

Jumping on him.

The Praetorian swung his Bladed Staff.

Blood and guts poured onto the cobblestones.

Warm blood coated his golden armour.

The Praetorian looked at the stage.

The woman saw him.

She was starting to leave.

The Praetorian slammed his Bladed Staff onto the ground.

A volley of bullets fired.

People screamed.

Running away.

Only to be stopped by the Praetorian Guards at the exits.

The Praetorian surged forwards.

People running away.

More people jumped him.

Thrusting blades at him.

The Praetorian jumped into the air.

Swinging his Bladed Staff with extreme martial prowess.

Nearby people were covered in the blood of their friends and family.

People roared in rage at him.

He did not care.

He was protecting the Empress.

The Praetorian was metres away from the stage.

A group of women stood around the stage to protect the woman in the purple cloak.

His target smiled at the Praetorian.

He stopped.

Gesturing for the women to move.

He did not want to kill them.

They thought he was denying the Empress' Will.

+Move!+ he roared into their minds.

They didn't move.

The woman in the purple cloak started to leave.

The Praetorian surge forward.

The women went to meet him.

They thrusted knives at him.

A few fired bullets.

He dodged the bullets with ease.

The Praetorian grabbed the women's wrists.

Snapping them.

The sound of shattering bone filled the air.

Followed by screams of agony.

The Praetorian did not kill them.

He kicked them to the ground.

Dashed up to the stage.

The woman in the cloak was gone.

He roared in rage.

He slammed his Bladed Staff onto the stage.

The wood cracked.

Someone tackled the Praetorian to the ground.

His armour scratching across the wood.

Pain pulsed through him.

The Praetorian rolled over.

A dagger came down towards his chest.

The Praetorian whacked the male attacker to the side.

Shattering his jaw.

As fast as lightning, the Praetorian climbed onto the man's back.

Grabbed his arm.

Pulled it back.

Ripping his arm from its socket.

He snapped the man's neck.

The broken neck showed a clear Raven tattoo.

Standing up, the Praetorian let out a deep breath.

He had failed.

The woman had escaped.

He might have captured thousands of ignorant people who choose to believe the woman's false words. And they would be interrogated by the Officers of Justice.

But who knew the damage his failure would do?

CHAPTER 6

Alvis and Aquene marched into a massive reception area with silver crystal walls with grand pieces of art on the wall. Showing Insenguard's stunningly beautiful forests and natural wonders.

Alvis looked around in disgust.

There was nothing here.

No furniture.

No plants.

No life.

Everything was clinically clean.

Waves of disappointment washed over Alvis. This was not the Insenguardian way.

Insenguard was about beauty, life and enjoyment.

And this clinical setting with a few pictures was not life filled and enjoyable.

Part of him wanted to go to the park afterwards and play on the swings to get some fun back in his old bones.

Yet Alvis was bewildered to why such a great, strong police force like the Lord Justice needed such a clinical appearance.

It was hardly the don't mess with us aura their officers give off.

If anything it gives an aura of please wait to be seated at your table.

The Chancellor could smell the thick layers of chemicals that were used to cleanse this place.

Additionally, Alvis hated the silence of the reception area.

There was literally no sound.

No humming.

No breathing.

Nothing.

Aquene tapped him.

Alvis frowned.

When he looked at her, Alvis noticed she was

pointing towards the end of the reception area.

He extended his neck.

To see a short well-dressed man holding a clipboard and parchment looking at them.

Alvis stated at him.

The most he stared the more he thought something like a spider was crawling over him.

His mouth begun to taste of Iron.

He looked away.

A part of Alvis wanted to walk away and leave this ugly place but he was here on a mission, not for himself. But for the Empress. It was his duty to be here.

Also, he was scared about what the Praetorian would do to him if he left.

The Chancellor and Aquene walked towards him.

He stood firm.

Writing on his parchment.

Aquene stared at this man, her eyes narrowed

Alvis crossed his arms.

The short man kept writing on his parchment.

Frowning upon the man, Alvis noticed his freshly ironed crisp white tunic with golden threads.

The man's hair was dirty blond and whilst his features would be considered young to many. Alvis judged the little mortal to be no younger than 35.

Both Alvis and Aquene looked at each other in disgust as they breathed in the strong wooden aftershave the man wore.

'Did he pour a bottle on himself' Aquene mouthed.

Alvis nodded.

The man still wrote on his parchment.

The Chancellor gave a loud cough.

"I know you are here, person,"

Aquene's mouth dropped.

"Excuse me, this is the Lord Chancellor of the Insenguardian Council. You will show him the respect he deserves,"

The man looked up.

His eyes widened as he looked at Aquene's beautiful slim body.

Alvis rolled his eyes.

"Son of Insenguard, please entertain my desire

for only a mere moment. Then I promise you can get back to your task," Alvis softly spoke.

Reluctantly, the man stopped writing and looked into the warm old eyes of the Chancellor.

"My Lord Chancellor, I am the Lord Justice's Personal Assistant. What do you need and make it quick?"

Aquene's mouth dropped a little more.

Alvis ignored the man's rude behaviour.

"All I require is to see the Lord Justice immediately,"

The Personal Assistant raised an eyebrow.

"Why do you think you are worth the Lord Justice's time?"

Aquene laughed out of pure shock.

"Because Son of Insenguard, I am the Chancellor of the Council and I am here on Council business. My authority is absolute on such matters. Now, please tell me where the Lord Justice is,"

The Assistant went back to writing on his clipboard.

Alvis and Aquene looked at one another.

Aquene gave the Chancellor a cheeky grin.

She walked up to the Assistant and slowly lowered the clipboard with her soft hands.

"Um, maybe we could get to know each other after you tell us," Aquene added.

The Assistant's face turned bright red.

Sweat poured down his face.

His eyes watered in confusion.

Alvis coughed a little as the sweat released more of the strong aftershave.

"Um, um, um. I'll go and see if I can find a location for you," the man said, running off.

Aquene stepped close to Alvis.

"Do you think he'll have a location for us?" she asked.

Alvis merely looked at her.

A heavy tapping sound echoed around the reception area.

Alvis turned around to see a large overweight man banging on the window.

"My Lord, please excuse me. I need to talk to this man,"

Alvis waved her away.

He cocked his head as Aquene hugged the man quickly and spoke to him.

His bones ached from standing up and walking too long without sitting down.

Yet his pain in his joints didn't bother him.

For this was only short term in the eyes of the Empress, and whatever pain he was feeling was surely nothing compared to the justice and truth he would discover for his Empress.

Although, rage flashed across Alvis' face as he was reminded that there were no chairs to sit on in the reception area.

Moments later, Aquene came back smiling.

It always warmed Alvis' heart to see the happiness of others.

"My Lord," Aquene greeted Alvis once more.

"Your friend is a magic user?" the Chancellor asked.

Aquene turned her head in surprise.

"Um, yes. How did you know?"

"The deep slice in his head is an Insenguardian magic bonding ritual. Where magical users literally bind their magic to the God Empress,"

"Um, yes. Anyway, Alvis. I presume the Assistant is not returning,"

A loud door slam echoed through the reception area.

"I take that as a no, Daughter of Insenguard,"

"Anyway, my friend used his magic to sense out the Lord Justice. He is in the swimming pool of the Insenguardian Palace,"

"Excellent work, Aquene,"

"Should we get going?"

"Of course, my dear. I just have one request first,"

"Anything, Alvis,"

"Can we please sit down for a few minutes?"

CHAPTER 7

Gliding through the door, the Praetorian marched into a large wooden bar.

Looking around with cold narrow eyes, the Praetorian saw the immense beams of wood cemented into one another to support the high domed roof. Which hundreds or perhaps thousands of lit candles hung down from on tiny silver wire.

The light from the candles made the wire dazzle and sparkle. Providing a pleasing atmosphere for the bar.

Still, the Praetorian sneered a little.

This was far from the Insenguardian way. Alcohol was a social drink and getting drunk was extremely frowned upon.

To the Praetorian and by extension the Empress, strongly believed a good mind is a strong mind.

Alcohol made the mind weak.

Although, the Praetorian did admire the Death Cult of Assassins beliefs around alcohol. Since in service to the Empress they refuse to drink. Yet the assassins always weaponise the alcohol of their foes.

Stepping into the bar, he started to get noticed.

Focusing on the people, the Praetorian clocked the white tunics of the guests with their large glasses of black Insenguardian wine.

Everyone was drinking in groups ranging from couples to families to entire departments at work.

Walking with his armoured boots pounding the wood floor, the Praetorian smelled the delicious spices and herbs used in the diners' meals.

He gave them a quick look.

Some had fresh Buffeater sliced in a thick buttery sauce.

Others had fruity soups.

Other people were enjoying sweet-smelling desserts.

The entire bar was more of a restaurant yet it was still a symphony of sweet, meaty and herby smells.

The Praetorian still didn't care.

Not whilst his mission was not complete.

Despite his mouth watering and the taste of earthy meats on his tongue, the Praetorian kept walking through the bar.

Everyone turned around on their royal blue crushed velvet covered chairs to look at him in his ornate golden armour.

People gasped.

People stared in awe.

Some people even cowered on the Praetorian's aura of devotion and power to the throne and the Empress.

Inside his armour, the Praetorian smiled a little. Pleased at himself for making these mortals cower in front of him.

These people were never his concern, only the Empress was.

When he got to the middle of the restaurant, he stopped.

Everyone stared at him.

The Praetorian turned his head.

He took off his helmet.

Everyone gasped at the sight of the Empress'

Praetorian.

Some people muttered prays of devotion to the Empress.

The Praetorian rolled his eyes at these Faithful people.

His eyes locked with a man in the far-right corner.

The Praetorian stormed towards him.

His face hardened.

His eyes turned icy cold.

Everyone kept watching the Praetorian.

He stopped dead in his tracks.

He looked down at the man.

Staring into the large black eyes of his target, the Praetorian took every little detail in about this man.

His large stocky frame and thick dark skin were covered in rough rags. He stank of toxic smoke and illegal highs.

The taste of burned flesh and tar filled the Praetorian's mouth.

The Target's face was youthful, maybe mid-twenties, multiple scars had twisted the forehead and cheeks of the man to make him look a lot old.

Frowning at the target's table, the Praetorian's disgust grew at the sight of large sticks of illegal substances and strange blue weeds piled high.

Standing up, the target smiled. Revealing rows upon rows of black shattered teeth.

The target gestured for the Praetorian to sit down as the target took his seat once more.

The Praetorian threw a drawing on the table.

Knocking over a pile of blue weed.

That knocked the choking smell of the toxic weed into the air.

The Praetorian coughed.

Snapping his helmet back on.

He waved the people behind him out.

Everyone complied.

The restaurant owner, a short woman, carefully yet quickly guided everyone out.

Out of kindness, the Praetorian unclipped a heavy large bag of gold coins from his waist.

He threw it at the owner.

Before waving her out.

The Praetorian pointed harshly to the highly detailed drawing on the table.

He emphasised the highly detailed raven tattoo on the parchment.

"YOU did this tattoo for everyone, didn't you!" the Praetorian demanded.

The man looked at him.

Sat back.

Crossed his arms.

The Praetorian whipped his Bladed Staff off his back.

Slamming it into the floor.

The wood cracked.

"Who else has the tattoo? What does it mean?"

The man was silent.

The Praetorian's blood started to boil.

He was not going to play any games.

Especially, with the Empress at risk.

This stupid mortal might be scum.

Yet he had information.

The Praetorian grinned a little.

With a thought, the blue weed was turned to ash.

The man's eyes widened.

He pushed into his chair.

The chair fell over.

The man's head smashed into the wooden floor.

The Praetorian stormed over.

Shattering the table.

He jabbed the Bladed Staff into the man's throat.

"Yes, I have magic, little mortal. I do not like to use it. I consider it cheating. Now, what does the tattoo mean?"

Nothing.

The Bladed Staff sliced the man's throat a little.

Tiny streams of blood trickled from the wound.

The Praetorian smiled.

"Raven, darkness. It means… um… I don't

know,"

The Praetorian went to push the Bladed Staff in deeper.

"No, wait. Please. A woman came. She wanted a design. It was… darkness. Yes. She wanted a design meaning darkness, evil. Um, I showed her a raven,"

Rage flashed over the Praetorian's face.

"Who was she!" he bellowed.

A tear ran down the mortal's face.

The Praetorian placed the Bladed Staff back on his back.

He grabbed the man by the throat.

"You mean nothing to me. You are scum. You are a cancer on Insenguard, on Her bringing your drugs into Her country. Tell me and you die quickly. Refuse to tell me, you will die in forty years and every day until then you will be begging for death,"

More tears flooded down the man's face.

"She will kill me,"

"If she kills you, it will be a lot less painful than forty years in agony,"

He nodded slowly.

"The woman. You know her. She wears the symbol of office. She is a Member of the Council. No, no, no. An Aide but she paid me. The parchment had a name on it…"

The man stopped.

"Tell me!"

"There was a name on the top corner of the parchment. It belonged to the Offices of the Lady Ajanta,"

"The Offices of the Village Representative," the Praetorian said, bitterly. "How far does this corruption go!"

The Praetorian threw him on the floor.

Whipped out his Bladed Staff.

Thrusted it through the man's throat.

Blood squirted into the air.

CHAPTER 8

Holding open the heavy crystal door to the swimming pool inside the Palace, Alvis let Aquene enter first.

Following their brief sit down at a local Insenguardian cafe, the two friends had formed a plan to deal with the Lord Justice.

Aquene stepped into the swimming pool chamber and Alvis walked behind her.

The Chancellor felt immense pleasure fill him as he glared upon the swimming pool.

Immensely strong rays of golden late afternoon sunlight shine through the enormous glass windows to the left of Alvis.

Causing the clean mineral water to sparkle like jewels in the light.

Alvis took a few steps forward to the edge of the

swimming pool.

The entire pool took up the entire chamber.

It was easily 100 metres long and 50 metres wide.

Pleasure continued to fill Alvis as he remembered the times where he loved swimming with his wife and son.

Those were the precious yet lost days.

A tear swelled in his eye.

One day, he knew he would rest and see them once again but until that moment when he deserved that chance. He knew he had the Empress' Work to do.

The sound of running water filled the air.

It made Alvis' old bladder want to release itself.

He ignored the sound.

Under the loudish sound of the mineral water being pumped into the pool. Alvis heard the splashing of someone swimming.

Ignoring the beauty of the bumpy rock walls of the pool, the Chancellor and Aquene fixed their eyes on the Lord Justice. Who swam up to them.

At the edge of the swimming pool, Alvis was

almost wrapped around in the golden light. Like an angel of justice and truth descending from the heavens.

The Lord Justice lifted himself out of the pool.

Water running off him.

Aquene made a sound of what could only be described as a cross between a gasp and excitement.

Alvis could understand her excitement.

Or at least infer to why Aquene was excited.

The Lord Justice stood up the pool water running down his abs and his muscles shone in the sunlight.

His chiselled body was matched by his long soaking brown hair and his strong jawline with strong facial features.

Alvis rolled his eyes at the Lord Justice as he smiled at Aquene.

The Lord Justice clearly knew how to use his sexuality.

The Lord Justice bent down to grab a long white towel to better cover himself up.

Since his short white undergarments didn't really work after they were wet.

Although, Alvis did see the Lord Justice had suffered a major burn and a deep cut on the right side of his face.

The Chancellor beamed a little at the thought of the Empress whacking the Lord Justice.

Equally, he was pretty surprised the Lord Justice would try something so forward.

The Lord Justice stepped towards the Chancellor.

Alvis felt the Lord Justice's body heat.

He was like a radiator.

Whilst the Lord Justice towered over Alvis. The Chancellor stared coldly into his gentle blue eyes.

The Lord Justice backed down.

"My Lord Chancellor, my Assistant warned me of your arrival. Yet I must question how you found me,"

Aquene was about to speak.

Alvis shot her a look.

"Fair, Son of Insenguard, I might not have a military background, but I have my ways. So, please tell me why you have not sent Officers to deal with the civil unrest,"

"Ah, I thought you wanted to discuss something more important,"

Aquene interrupted: "You are a Member of the Council. It is your duty to…"

The Lord Justice dropped the towel and slide back into the pool.

Making a point to flex his muscles at Aquene.

She ignored him.

Her eyes narrowed in rage.

The Lord Justice's mouth dropped.

Alvis gave a brief chuckle.

This must have been the first time… well after dealing with the Empress, his second time in his life where his body had failed to silence woman and men.

"As I was saying, it is your duty to protect and police Insenguard,"

"I'm sorry, Chancellor. This is not my problem and who is this woman to talk to me this way,"

"Ha, Mighty Son. She is my Aide, and she has every right to ask these questions. So, my dear, please tell me when you will send in officers?"

"I will not. This is not a job for my Officers of Justice. No crimes have been committed,"

Alvis' mouth dropped.

"Come now, Noble Son of Insenguard. There are have been attacks, deaths and robberies. These are serious crimes to the throne and the Empress,"

The Lord Justice just looked at him and smiled.

"If there are attacks then it falls under the jurisdiction of the Grand Master of the Homeland,"

Alvis gave a large evil smile.

Finally, the Chancellor had an answer.

"Oh, Son of Insenguard. Now, that is clever. You knew there would be attacks sooner or later and the law clearly states it is up to the Homeland Division of the military to deal with attacks on Insenguardian soil,"

The Lord Justice nodded.

"Um, so you want our people to die and suffer? The Homeland is a military fraction of the Council. They will KILL the attackers. You could save lives here," Aquene pointless said.

Alvis knelt down the swimming pool titles.

His knees clicking.

He placed his old fingers on the back of the neck of the Lord Justice.

His smooth wet skin feeling weird in Alvis' gasp.

"Might Son, my dearest Lord Justice, you do not have to send in your Officers if you don't want to. I will request the Homeland Division does it. Then when I send my report to the Empress. I will explain how the Homeland were the mighty heroes of this battle,"

The Lord Justice tensed.

"My dearest Aquene, do you think the Empress will give the Grand Master of the Homeland a celebration feast, medals and perhaps even a room in her palace?"

"Oh, of course, she will Chancellor. You know what I've heard she gives unlimited access to her private gym, fighting cages and swimming pool to her favourite warriors,"

"That is true, my dear. But I am afraid that I will have to go and tell the Grand Master about the situation. I hope he gets the glory he deserves,"

The Chancellor went to get up.

He gestured to Aquene for help.

She rushed over.

"Mighty Son of Insenguard, it was a pleasure talking to you. The Empress Protects,"

Alvis and Aquene started to walk away.

"Wait, I'll send in my Officers,"

CHAPTER 9

The evening sun was a red fiery orb in the redding sky sending bright orange rays of light into the drawing room as the Praetorian marched in.

He looked around carefully.

All around him tens of elegantly dressed women in long silky Royal purple dresses and men in posh fancy black suits stood there chatting. Drinking the Village Representative's fine black Insenguardian wine.

Stealthily, gliding through the crowd, the Praetorian felt the soft red rugs under his feet.

Allowing him to glide silently across the floor.

The Praetorian wanted to shake his head at the ignorance of these people for not noticing him, and being too consumed by their idol chatter.

However, a few people gave him some poorly

times looks. The Praetorian allowed his stone war hardened face to show a little smile.

These people were true Insenguardians.

The Empress had always said to her people the best way to surprise someone is to trick them.

That is exactly what these new Insenguardians had done.

Continuing gliding through the crowd, the Praetorian pretended to admire the grand murals of Insenguardian battles with spiky demons, vampires, tree monsters and more unspeakable horrors with the so-called God Empress being a mighty golden warrior leading her people in the centre.

This mural stretched all around the large drawing table with there being nothing on the wall to cover up a piece of this mural. That was meant to be an accurate historical retelling.

The Praetorian doubted the validity of that claim yet he had other things to deal with.

As he glided past one couple, the taste of fresh juicy fish filled his mouth and citrus smells filled the air.

He gave a quick look at the food the couple were eating.

He raised an eyebrow not knowing what it was.

It was something between a slice of white fish on a square cracker and a paste on some thin bread.

With a final step, the Praetorian stopped.

Studying the surrounding crowd.

He remembered why they were tricking him.

None of them were talking or drinking.

It looked like it.

People raised glasses to mouth.

Yet none drank the black wine.

He studied them.

They studied him.

He tensed.

He was ready to use his Bladed Staff if needed.

After a moment, they stopped talking.

The drawing room went silent.

Two women walked towards the Praetorian.

Nodding all the other men and women in the room to continue speaking and actually drinking.

Staring at the women with contempt, the Praetorian saw these two tall women in bright purple velvet dresses.

The one to the Praetorian's right was wearing a thick twisted golden necklace with a golden raven in the middle.

The Praetorian stared with rage.

He looked up at the woman's face.

Frowning the Praetorian, focused on those hard-stunning features that caused men to fall under her spell as her youthful beauty stunned them.

Her attraction was aided by her large curves as well.

She gave the Praetorian a seductive smile.

He did not care.

This only made him more rageful.

Yet he composed himself.

He was the Empress' Praetorian.

He was Her Left Hand and he needed to act like it.

Lashing out here would achieve nothing.

He knew who she was.

This woman was Ajanta, People's Representative

on the Council of Insenguard. A supposed woman of the people.

A supposed contrast to the other people on the Council who had a military background.

The Praetorian stretched his fingers.

Ajanta whipped out her hair.

Her long black hair fanned out.

The drawing room filled with the scent of coconut.

"Oh Praetorian, you came. Oh my Lord, this is brilliant," Ajanta said.

The Praetorian continued to frown.

"I must confess People's Representative…"

"Oh Praetorian, please, call me Ajanta,"

"People's Representative," he said firmly. "I did not expect you to know the Insenguardian ways yet. You knew the second I was here,"

"Oh my Praetorian, oh. For such a strong, muscular man, and your size of course. I'm ever so impressed by you. The way you sneaked into the entrance, the living room and upstairs without anyone seeing you is very impressive. Let me show you my gratitude,"

She leant forward.

The other woman grabbed her before she signed her own death warrant.

The Praetorian gave a subtle nod of thanks to the other woman.

"Oh, really, Aide. I wanted to show the Praetorian a loving time,"

The Praetorian had had enough.

"Who is in charge of your office supplies?" he demanded.

Ajanta looked seductively at him.

"Oh, Praetorian. I could never get these nails damaged,"

The Representative ran her long black nails down the Praetorian's armoured chest to his lower stomach.

The Praetorian bit his tongue back hard.

He wanted to smash this woman's skull in.

"My Lord Praetorian, I am in charge of the Office supplies,"

"Then in Her name, I must talk to you," he commanded with great authority to the other woman.

He looked at the Representative. "In private!"

"Oh Praetorian, you know what they say three are better than two,"

"Out!" the Praetorian screamed.

Everyone charged out of the drawing room.

He snapped his neck around.

Staring coldly at the other woman.

She tensed.

Her slim figure shock in fear.

Sweat damped her dress.

The Praetorian smiled a little.

"You are the Representative's Aide,"

"Yes, my Lord,"

"Good,"

Together they wandered over to the large window in the centre of the mural in front of them.

The floor squeaked as they walked.

Looking out the window, the Praetorian saw children playing, laughing and the crowd from the drawing room poured out of the building.

"Why did you pay for the tattoos?"

The Aide shot the Praetorian a look of anger.

"That is none of the Empress' business,"

"I am the Empress' Praetorian. Everything that is Her business is my business,"

"That is still none of Her business,"

"You are Her subject. Everything is subject to the Empress' Will and Ever Watchful Presence,"

"The tattoos are meaningless,"

The children outside stopped laughing.

"Tell that to the people I have killed who bare that tattoo,"

The Aide was silent.

"The tattoo is the only link I have to these attacks and these traitors,"

The children in the street ran away.

The Aide's voice changed.

Becoming more confident.

"Traitors, my Lord?" she smiled.

"You!"

He recognised the voice.

The street was empty outside.

He grabbed the woman.

Ripping off her dress sleeves.

The raven tattoo was carved by knife into her flesh.

She smiled.

"Who are you working for?"

There was no one and nothing outside the building.

"Who!" the Praetorian screamed.

Hundreds of cloaked figures with torches marched outside.

A bullet shattered the window's glass.

The Aide's head exploded.

Fireballs screamed through the air outside.

Smashing into the building.

The building became engulfed in flames.

The Praetorian ran to the door.

More fires engulfed the doorway.

CHAPTER 10

Alvis stormed into the meeting chamber.

His face furious.

Aquene rushed behind him.

Nobody paid attention to the Master of the Meeting.

To the other 5 members of the Council standing there talking. The Chancellor was just a ghost and something to be ignored.

Alvis bones might have ached and pain pulsed through him from his overly fast walk. Yet he had a job to do.

He breathed out slowly.

The pain stopped a little.

Looking at the members of the Council, Alvis

raised his eyebrows as these strong heroic people were acting like children.

Even now, with Insenguard in turmoil, these heroes still fail to see eye to eye and come together for the greater good.

That was the greatest shame Alvis believed. Not the infighting or the lack of respect for one another but the inability for them to do the right thing when it mattered most.

Glazing around the immense meeting chamber with its white oak walls and flooring.

The Chancellor saw each of the Members arguing around the massive rectangular blackwood table with 8 large golden leather chairs underneath.

He stepped towards his chair at the head of the table.

His feet squeaked on the freshly waxed golden floor.

No one could hear Alvis' speaking over the shouting.

As he slowly lowered himself into his seat, Alvis focused on each Member from left to right.

The People's Representative wore her long bright purple dress with her golden necklace that sparkled in the bright candle light of the chandelier.

Alvis frowned at her curves and her inappropriate slice in the front of her dress.

He knew a bunch of servants had wanted to stay for the meeting for the sole purpose of watching her.

The Chancellor quickly dismissed all servants from the meeting chamber.

That was one reason.

The other reason was Alvis was prepared, if needed, to take some drastic action and the fewer witnesses the better.

Alvis did not want to, but he was serving his Empress.

Next Alvis looked at the Lord Justice who wore an extremely tight uniform and he subtly flexed to the other Members.

The Chancellor turned to look at Aquene.

Her face quickly turned to disgust at the Lord Justice.

The Emissary shouting cause Alvis' attention as she screamed at the Lord of Iron for something to do with oil stains on her bedsheets.

The Chancellor fixed his eyes on the Lord of Iron, the representative on the Council for the Lord Forge Master.

Alvis wasn't really sure what that meant. Something to do with Insenguard's weapon factories, he thought.

However, a spike in his chair rapidly pulsed stabbing pain in his back.

Therefore, he didn't really care.

He needed to find that damn maintenance person and give him a tour of everything that needed fixing!

Alvis gave Aquene a quick hand gesture.

She whipped out a gun.

Fired it.

Dropped it.

The Chancellor coughed at the smell of gunpowder.

Everyone broke into combat positions.

Alvis laughed.

Next he gestured everyone to take a seat.

Sneering at each other, each Member reluctantly took their seat around the table.

Alvis gave each of the Members a smile and nod of respect.

The spike dug into him a little more.

He wanted to cry a little.

"Fair Children of Insenguard..." the Chancellor began.

"Chancellor, how dare you activate your emergency powers, and legally force us to convene a meeting," The Lord Justice barked. Giving a seductive wink to Aquene.

"Now, now, fair children of Insenguard, you have all forced my hand. Now, do we know where the Representative of the Covert Military Division is or the Praetorian?"

The Grand Master of the Homeland spoke "Negative, Lord Chancellor. All reports are struggling to find the Covert Representative, and the Praetorian was last seen..."

"By me," the People Representative began. "Oh Chancellor, oh. I'm ever so worried about that strong Praetorian. Oh, I hope he's okay. Oh, oh, that poor man,"

Aquene walked up to stand next to Alvis.

He waved her to speak.

"What do you know?"

The Lord Justice licked his lips at her.

"Oh, Alvis. Oh. You let your Side speak. How nice of you. Oh, Alvis," She said. "I left him with my Side then those awful people with torches came. I think he's trapped inside the burning building. Oh, I hope he's okay, "

The Chancellor lent back in his chair.

Sending the spike deep into his back.

"So fair and noble members of the Council, you were all arguing and shouting at each other whilst we have an entire region burning and two missing Members,"

They nodded without shame nor remorse.

Alvis shook his head.

"It matters not what you did before, Fair Children. Now we must look to the future so Lord Justice report,"

The Lord Justice gave a seductive wink to Aquene.

She looked to the Chancellor.

He shook his head. Knowing she wanted to scream curses and belittle his overly sexual ways.

He was a womaniser. It was as simple as that.

Alvis made a note of the Lord Justice crossing the final line.

He would deal with him later, he was sure.

"Lord Justice!" the Grand Master of the Homeland bellowed.

"Ah, you people again. This is not my concern. I don't care if these people march and protest,"

"Well, it is certainly not under my jurisdiction. The Homeland Military Division is responsible for defending the Homeland from external threats. It is the job of the Justice Officers to protect the Homeland internally,"

The Chancellor nodded.

"Come, come, dear Son of Insenguard, send out your Officers to protect us, and most importantly keep the Empress' subjects safe,"

The Lord Justice sneered.

"Oh, Justice, oh. Please. Please. Send out your forces. You can unleash your forces on me if you want,"

Alvis's eyes widened.

He looked to Aquene.

She was equally speechless.

"Um, Policing is not my concern," the Lord Justice shot out.

Alvis rolled his eyes at the stupidity of it all.

He wanted nothing more than to execute these people right now for incompetence.

Alvis had the power to do that. Yet he was a patient man.

His flaw.

Yet he was patient.

"Dearest Lord Justice, explain to the Council why after our chat earlier you only dispatched 20% of your Officers to deal with the riots,"

The Lord Justice stretched.

His muscular chest bungled and rippled.

"This again, Alvis,"

Alvis slammed his fists on the table.

"That is Lord Chancellor to you. I have been placed in position by the highest authority of the Empress. Now, you will explain yourself, or I will use every little piece of my power to force you to comply!"

Everyone stared at Alvis.

Then they looked at each other.

Their eyes wide.

Clearly, shocked the old man had it in him.

"What legal power?" the Lord Justice questioned. "I am the law of Insenguard. I control the courts, the laws and…"

"Shut up you womaniser," Aquene snapped.

All Members on the Council gave her a subtle nod of approval.

"As the Law, you should know I can requisition fractions of Insenguard. I can pose a vote that goes on public record and if I win. That fraction falls under my direct command,"

The Lord Justice fell silent.

"Now, Son of Insenguard, we have a Praetorian in danger, and I intend to help him. Send out ALL your Justice Officers and suppress the riots,"

"I will," he muttered.

"What did you say, Child?"

"I will send out my forces, Lord Chancellor,"

"Thank you,"

Aquene cocked her head in surprise.

Alvis knew how to work a room.

The Chancellor felt an immense sense of pride wash over him.

He turned to look at the Grand Master of the Homeland.

"Fair and wonderous Grand Master, may I request you send in three squads of Insenguardian warriors to support the Officers?"

"Of course, my Lord Chancellor,"

"Excellent. Thank you,"

The Lord Justice muttered something unpleasant.

"Everyone dismissed," Alvis ordered. "We have a country to save,"

CHAPTER 11

Flames flooded the doorway.

Cutting the Praetorian off.

The flames on the outside of the building continued to dance across the building.

The mural wall around the drawing room started to turn black as the heated bricks started to burn the paint.

Thin black smoke filled the drawing room.

He coughed.

The smoke slowly became thicker.

Immediately, the Praetorian sealed his golden helmet to his ornate armour.

The Praetorian allowed a little smile to break his hard lips.

He had time.

The magical bacteria inside his armour would give him oxygen.

In addition, the Empress' magical protection should prevent his armour from getting too hot.

He had time.

He needed to focus.

Why did this happen?

Why did the killer kill the Aide when the Praetorian spoke to her?

Why not before or after?

And why burn the place down?

These were all urgent questions that the Praetorian needed to answer.

However, he needed to escape first.

The large colourful mural of the Empress battling alongside her Insenguardian Sons and Daughters started to burn and blacken.

Grand columns of smoke poured from thick patches of paint.

Even through his helmet's air filter, the Praetorian could smell the immense toxic smoke.

The flames at the door started to consume the floor as it edged into the drawing room.

Bright green flames shot into the air, as the fire started to chomp away at the fire retarded floor.

An explosion threw him forward.

He landed hard into the wooden floor.

His metal heated up.

His fingers burned.

Pain shot through him.

He looked up.

The bright green flames danced towards him.

Swirling, twirling as they came to consume him.

He jumped up.

The Roaring fire got louder.

Turning around, the Praetorian saw the flames centimetres from his face.

He jumped up.

However, the Praetorian knew he had time.

He needed to focus.

The Empress did not raise him out of the

slumbers of his homeland to be useless in this moment.

The Praetorian took a heavy toxic, black smoke-filled breath.

Then he released it.

Scanning the drawing room, he noticed the body of the Aide.

He rushed over.

Studying the body, the Praetorian pressed his hot metal fingers into her shattered head.

The flesh was still warm.

Slowly, being cooked by the fire.

After a few seconds of flicking around fleshy bone. He found the bullet site.

He paused.

The Praetorian scratched his forehead.

His stomach flipped.

Even his lunch wanted to come back up.

Carefully, the Praetorian found the fragments of the bullet that killed the Aide.

It confirmed his suspicions.

He held a special type of sniper bullet that only Insenguardian snipers had access to.

Someone within the military was behind this attack.

The Praetorian's hands formed fists.

This was the worst sort of treachery.

Not only had these new citizens been blinded into outrageous beliefs by a false woman. Yet true Insenguardian warriors had turned from the Empress' light.

The Praetorian swore multiple times under his breath.

Searing pain filled his boots.

He jumped into the air.

Bright green flames engulfed the entire chamber now.

The Praetorian's entire vision was filled with dancing, swirling, whirling green flames.

They licked his armour.

Small dense columns of pitch black smoke poured into the drawing room.

Then the Praetorian realised what the explosion had been.

He stopped.

Focusing on a single detail.

In front of him was a massive smouldering hole from a mortar blast.

These traitors had mortar cannons at their disposal.

The crackling fire got louder and louder.

The Praetorian screamed as the flames engulfed his armour.

Apart of him wanted to stand still.

Allowing the flames to claim him.

He had protected the Emperor and Empress for years.

Insenguard might have fallen and the Praetorian might have failed to protect the Emperor.

Yet he was not going to let his Daughter the Empress die.

His skin started to cook.

An immense psychic pressure pressed into his mind.

That is when it became clear.

The Empress needed him.

The Praetorian could not, would not rest yet.

His head turned to the hole from the mortar blast.

He couldn't see through it.

It could be a three metre drop to the ground.

Or a 50 metre drop.

He didn't know.

He did not care.

Not when in service to the Empress.

The Praetorian had what he needed.

He had some proof on the traitors.

And that is what he needed for his Empress.

He charged and jumped out of the hole.

CHAPTER 12

Alvis awoke as Aquene slammed another pile of reports down on the large smooth wooden reading table.

Dust was kicked into the air.

The Chancellor's eyes opened startled.

He sneezed repeatedly.

Stretching his aching bones, Alvis ran his fingers briefly across the wooden reading table.

The lumps and bumps still warm from were he had been sleeping for the past hour.

While Aquene had diligently hunted down books and reports from the bookshelves.

Alvis gave her an extremely apologetic smile.

He felt awful.

He had dragged her along to this place of books and left her to do all the work.

That was not how Alvis wanted to be regarded.

He was not some fragile man who needed a carer.

Alvis was a dedicated servant of the Empress.

Aquene grabbed his hand and squeezed it gently.

A sharp pain shot up his arm.

Yet he didn't mind.

This woman, this kind gentle woman was a great Aide and probably the only person he could call friend in this new country.

Aquene started humming a merry little tune to herself.

The Chancellor beamed at the young woman as the sweet merry humming reminded him of his beautiful wife when they first met all those decades ago.

Alvis stood up and stretched.

He turned around to see the lines upon lines of books that were probably tens of metres tall.

The thick red leather covers of the books made Alvis' heart skip, reminding him of his children and

Gauic grand library.

Yet he had never seen something as grand as this library. There must have been over a million books in here.

Then Alvis' mind wandered to the horrific thought about Insenguard's forbidden texts.

Part of Alvis hoped the rumours were lies.

Although, the Chancellor knew Insenguard had a dark side.

Even the moonlight shining through the immense glass roof of the Library, that added a magical beauty to the candle light, couldn't hide the darkness beneath Insenguard.

Alvis subtly rubbed his heart at the thought of coming face to face with such truth.

He might have faced evil in Gauic, but Insenguard was a country of demon hunters and the hunters of evil, so only the Empress would know the true extent of what Insenguard has in its vaults and dungeons.

A few nights ago, Alvis woke up to hear the immense sound of something screaming in pure agony. It was nothing he had told himself.

But what if it wasn't?

Alvis shook the dark thoughts away.

Turning away from the beautiful sight of thousands of books, Alvis returned his attention to the pile of books and reports in front of him.

Sitting back down on the hard iron chair, Alvis gestured Aquene to pass him a report.

She complied.

When he grabbed the report, the rough green leather cover felt strangely smooth in his weak grip.

He opened it.

Aquene gagged.

Alvis laughed, and breathed in the smell of old parchment.

"I am sorry, my dear. I did not mean to go to the land of dreams,"

"It's okay, Alvis. We've all been there. Now, what are we looking for?"

Alvis opened another report.

"We are looking for the location of the Representative for Convert Military Division, my dear,"

"Well, I've checked with my friends in the Homeland Division and they're focused on something else at the moment,"

"What fair child? The riots?"

Aquene looked to see if anyone else was around.

She leant in close to Alvis.

"There are reports that a sizable force of Gauic soldiers are gathering within striking distance of Insenguard,"

Alvis straightened his back and rubbed his forehead.

"That is strange, my dear. What did the Emissary have to say?"

Aquene smiled.

"No one can find her. Otherwise, the Grand Master of the Homeland and the Emissary would attempt to get the Gauic to stand down,"

Alvis's eyebrows rose.

"Something is happening, my dear. Something is happening and it is up to us to find out what. Especially, with the Praetorian missing,"

Aquene nodded.

"Alvis, I reached out to a friend in the Death Cult of Assassins who has a kill team in Insenguard…"

"What Fair Daughter? I didn't think the Assassins were allowed to operate in the Homeland?"

Aquene gave him a cheeky smile.

"And she said the job of her Kill team is to monitor the other fractions,"

Alvis led in closer.

His eyes fixated on Aquene.

"The Kill team reported the Covert Representative has been missing for days. Coming and going. Even now, they do not have a location for any of the twenty Covert soldiers,"

"My dearest Aquene, are you telling me even the Assassins, the Empress' best hunters cannot find twenty ruthless, brutal hunters?"

Aquene nodded.

A drop of sweat poured off her forehead.

Alvis laughed a little.

This was ridiculous.

How could so many people turn from the Empress' light?

The same light who gave them hope and a new home.

"Alvis, why would the Covert people turn traitor?"

The Chancellor coughed a little. Taken by her comment.

"Um, my dear, we do not…"

Aquene looked at him, gesturing to the reports.

"Fine, Fair and wonderful Aquene, it is most probable the Covert Military Division are traitors and heretics to the Empress,"

Aquene was shaking a little now.

Alvis placed a gentle fragile hand on her's.

He rubbed it.

Sending light earthy perfume into the air.

"Fair Daughter of Insenguard, look at me,"

Aquene lifted up her head and stared into Alvis' old glassy eyes.

"We are the Chosen of the Empress. It was by Her Will, my dear, that we were placed in this position. She will Protect us. In return, we must act in Her interests,"

Aquene nodded slowly.

"What do we do now?"

Alvis paused.

He had never had to deal with traitors before.

Even when he was in Gauic, he was the traitor- so this was completely new territory.

"You must go to the Grand Master of the Homeland, my dear. Tell him of our findings. I will go and find the Praetorian,"

She took a deep breath in and out.

"Aquene, my friend. We will be fine,"

A bullet screamed through the air.

Exploding Aquene's head.

CHAPTER 13

Jumping out of the large hole in the wall, the Praetorian quickly fell through the air.

He landed hard on the soft ground below.

Snapping out his Bladed Staff, he looked around.

Thick black smoke poured around him from the burning building he had jumped from.

All around him, the fire roared with rage as it chomped and crackled through the building.

Consuming all it touched.

The fire had spread to other buildings.

The entire area was engulfed in cleansing, all-consuming flames.

They roared and crackled together in a grand symphony of destruction.

A few people screamed in pain as the flame melted their flesh before consuming them.

The Praetorian turned his head around.

He only saw the bright red and green flames swirling and dancing in the wind, with thick black smoke rising into the sky.

On the back of his armour, the Praetorian felt the searing heat of the fire started to lick and tickle him.

The Praetorian stamped his foot down in frustration.

He had failed once again.

He needed the Aide alive to tell him about the plot.

Yet he had failed to do that.

The Praetorian's blood began to boil.

He was slipping.

Maybe not in the eyes of the Empress, his Lord and Master.

But definitely in his eyes.

How was he meant to lead the noble Praetorian Guard if he couldn't complete simple tasks?

The Praetorian frowned at the sight of these burning buildings.

Not because he cared for the buildings or the people burning inside of them. That was not the job of a Praetorian, but he was furious at these traitors.

Burning and using fire was cowardice in the eyes of the Praetorian Guard.

Better to die in the fires of melee combat then kill by lighting a match.

Anyone could do that.

Not everyone can kill in melee.

Stepping forward, the thick black smoke warped around the Praetorian.

In the distance, the Praetorian heard the screams of people being slaughtered by sword and bullet.

He prepared to strike with his Bladed Staff.

Stepping out of the smoke, nobody noticed him.

Despite, the Praetorian's golden ornate armour. He was invisible as far as the traitors were concerned.

In front of him, the Praetorian saw men and women dressed in white tunics ran after innocent people with immense swords and guns.

After hatching them to death.

The smell of gunpowder and vapourised blood filled the air.

Whatever falsehoods these mortals had been promised, the Praetorian vowed to kill these mortals for them.

For this was an assault on the Empress and Her true words. She would not want Insenguardian brother turning on brother nor Sisters.

Insenguard was a nation of One.

There were no others or divisions in this nation.

The Praetorian growled a little in fury.

He may not care for these mortals and their lives. Yet he cared for the Empress and Her work.

These people were nothing more than taint upon Her work.

The Praetorian charged.

Smashing the skull of one man.

He ripped his Bladed Staff out of the head of the man.

Blood spattered everywhere.

The Praetorian laughed.

Another man charged at him.

He swung his Bladed Staff.

It ripped into the stomach of the man.

His bones and stomach popped.

Cracking bones filled the air.

A volley of bullet dented the Praetorian's armour.

He spun around.

A group of men and women fired once more.

The Praetorian dived out the way.

He charged at them.

Swinging his Bladed Staff.

Some people dodged it.

Others had their skulls shattered.

Someone leapt onto the Praetorian.

Thrusting a knife in-between his helmet and armour.

The Praetorian swore.

He grabbed the person.

Ripping them over his armour.

Before snapping their back over his knees.

Fluids spattered over his chest plate.

The person's gun dropped to the floor.

More footsteps charged at him.

The Praetorian dived out the way.

Jumped up.

Firing a volley of shots at the new incoming foes.

A group of men hit the ground.

Blood pouring out from them.

Pain flooded the Praetorian's body.

He remembered the blade forced into his armour.

He pulled it out.

Blood trickled out of the wound.

Each time the Praetorian moved his right arm. Pain filled him.

The Praetorian was thrown to the floor.

A tall brutish man rapidly punched the

Praetorian's face.

The smell of sweat from the brutal man was horrific.

The Praetorian headbutted the man.

Cracking his skull open.

The brutal man dropped to the floor.

Blood poured down the outside of the Praetorian's helmet.

Pushing himself back up, the Praetorian frowned. Rubbing his forehead.

Everyone was gone.

All slaughtered, hacked-up bodies were left around him.

A clicking started to fill the street.

The Praetorian cocked his head.

He knew the sound.

It was a sort of country wide communication system designed by the Empress' father.

The Praetorian had no idea how it worked, nor did he care.

However, he knew it was something about the

Empress' magic and it allowed the speaker to transmit messages all over the country.

A harsh voice began "People of Insenguard, we have been abandoned for the last time. The Empress promised you hope and a new life, and in less than a week she has abandoned you,"

The Praetorian gripped his Bladed Staff tight.

This was treachery plain and simple.

"Well, fear not, Insenguardians. I am the Representative of the Covert Military Division on the Council of Insenguard,"

The Praetorian smiled a little.

He finally had a name.

Something to start with.

That hope quickly died.

"Me and my mighty allies on the Council will deliver you from the Empress' treachery and we will give you the life you deserve,"

His friends?

The Praetorian started walking quickly.

He didn't know where.

It was pitch black.

No one was on the street.

He kept listening.

"I, the Lord Justice, the Emissary and two others will deliver you. So, please citizens of Insenguard take up arms and join us. Come to the Cathedral of the Emperor, wait outside and let us join arms in this fight for our freedom!"

The Praetorian grinned with murderous intent.

Partially, he couldn't believe the arrogance of the traitors.

They had just told him where to kill them all.

He charged towards the Cathedral.

Ready to end this treachery.

He stopped.

"Praetorian, I know you're listening. You might want to check on the Chancellor. You might be able to save him yet,"

CHAPTER 14

The bullet screamed through the air.

Aquene's head exploded. Her beautiful young head cracked like an egg as the Bullet exploded.

The gunshot echoed louder around the enormous library with its millions off red leather-covered books on the high shelves.

A thick cloud rich red vaporised blood drifted across the air.

While thick dark red slashes of blood spattered across the large wooden reading table.

The blood turned the pile of reports and books red.

Their pages turned to red mush.

Before a little piece of the mush seeped onto the table.

The rest of Aquene's head landed with a loud thump on the table.

As her headless body whacked the table, Alvis thought he heard a few ribs cracking.

He knew he was in danger.

But a part off him didn't care.

Alvis just kept looking at Aquene's body.

He placed his fingers on his forehead.

A tear welled up in his eye.

His only true friend was dead.

Murdered at the hand of a coward who wasn't even brave enough to show themselves.

How disgustingly dishonourable.

Alvis had hated the so-called honour killing of Gauic yet in that moment, he understood.

For a brief second, he understood why the feral tribes of Gauic massacred each other for honour.

This was wrong.

It was fundamentally disgusting that such a gentle woman had been taken from him.

Maybe she reminded him of a child he never had. Whatever the answer, or why he cared so much for her. It didn't matter.

It only mattered that she died for something.

Alvis allowed his rage to manifest.

He promised himself to leave violence and bloodshed behind him when he left Gauic.

But this had changed things.

He needed to act when the time was right.

Returning his attention to the lifeless headless Aquene, Alvis noticed how the blood had dried slightly around her shattered neck and jaw.

The air was still thick with the smell of blood and gunpowder.

Even the candle light made Aquene's body look creepy.

Alvis tilted his head back.

His stomach rumbled.

The Chancellor looked at the cool peaceful night sky through the glass domed roof.

One day he would be at peace with his family.

But he had a mission to complete first.

Breathing out slowly to manage the pain from aching bones, Alvis stood and kissed Aquene's lifeless hand.

He heard footsteps coming up behind him.

Avis turned around to see the People's Representative in her long tight-fitting black dress walk towards him holding a large pistol.

The Chancellor tensed.

Behind her, Alvis saw the Lord of Iron walked towards him.

The Lord's mechanical twisted humanoid form was an abomination to see. With his large metal cables pumping oil around his body and grand metal claws instead of hands.

The horrific smell of burnt black oil field the air.

"What is this, Daughter of Insenguard!" Alvis demanded.

"Oh, Alvis. Oh. This is the future. This is the start of a new beginning. Oh, Alvis. We are going to have so much fun together,"

Alvis continued to tense.

"Oh Alvis, even as we speak. My allies are announcing the Empress' treachery and we will lead our people into a new golden age,"

"Ha, you are deluded Former Daughter of

Insenguard. It is not the Empress who is the traitor. It is you and your conspirators. You will never win. The other members of the Council will not submit,"

The Lord of Iron threw a severed head on the table.

Alvis gasped.

Gripping the material over his heart.

The head belonged to the Grand Master of the Homeland.

"Oh, Alvis. We tried to recruit him. Oh, he was fun. He refused so I killed him. Don't make the same mistake,"

The Chancellor stared into the cold lifeless eyes of the Grand Master of the Homeland.

Fear gripped him.

These traitors were serious killers.

Alvis truly believed at that moment that these people would do anything to claim Insenguard for themselves.

Yet he was still alive.

Aquene was dead.

But Alvis was alive, and he needed to use that to

his advantage.

He stumbled towards the People's Representative.

"Fair Daughter of Insenguard, please tell me why you are doing this?"

"Oh, Alvis it is simple. The Empress has turned her back on us. So, we will do the same to Her,"

The Chancellor felt a wave of warmth pass through him.

He did not know why he felt it, but he was convinced it was a signal from the Empress.

She had not abandoned him.

He will not abandon Her.

Although, he felt something else.

Almost like the Praetorian was coming for him.

Alvis knew exactly what needed to be done.

He needed time.

"Um, So, dearest people, why do you believe the Empress has turned on you?"

She did not answer.

"Okay, Fair and Beautiful Daughter, what are

your demands? I know you have them,"

She smiled at him.

The People's Representative ran a seductive hand down the Chancellor's chest and stomach.

"We want the Empress to come under the jurisdiction of the Council of Insenguard. We control Her. We want to say when she can leave and come back. We want to say who she can kill and cannot,"

"Ha, Daughter of Insenguard. That is ridiculous. The Empress is the only world leader who cares about other countries, world peace and Her own people. That is why she has left us now. She has left us to better Insenguard for the long term, and Insenguard has been rebuilt in the space of a week. That is impressive. It is our job as Council Members…"

"Oh, Alvis. Do not be all high and mighty with me. We will control the entire thing and the Gauic forces will help us,"

Alvis froze.

Insenguard was about to be invaded.

The Homeland division of the military was leaderless.

Insenguard was facing a civil war.

The Empress was gone.

The majority of the Council were traitors.

Alvis knew it was up to him and if the Praetorian lived, then it would be up to both of them to save Insenguard.

The People's Representative looked at Alvis.

She smiled.

Then she frowned.

She whacked him across the face.

Alvis fell.

Hitting his hips on the edges of the reading table.

Pain flooded his senses.

He fell to the floor.

The Lord of Iron pressed a cold heavy metal boot onto his chest.

"The Empress Protects," Alvis muttered.

The Lord of Iron hummed a little as the archaic metal started to activate.

The air crackled loudly with magical energy.

Alvis stared into the black eyes of the Lord of

Iron.

There was no emotion nor remorse.

Alvis was going to die, and nobody was going to care.

His lungs started to burn as they gasped for air.

"Oh, stop!" the People's Representative demanded.

In a rough, non-human voice, the Lord of Iron barked: "Negative,"

"Oh, Lord, oh. Stop. Our magic ally has detected the Praetorian. We must leave and come back with reinforcements,"

The Lord of Iron kept pressing down.

He stopped.

"Chancellor!" the Praetorian shouted from the far end of the library.

The People's Representative blew Alvis a kiss and both traitors left quickly.

Alvis pushed his head up.

He saw the Praetorian in his mighty golden ornate armour run towards him.

The Praetorian scanned the area with his Bladed Staff.

Ready to strike.

"Help me up, Son of Insenguard,"

The Praetorian rolled his eyes.

Before, helping Alvis up.

The Chancellor bit his tongue as immense pain radiated from his battered hips and leg joints.

"Come now, Chancellor. We must leave,"

"No, my dear. They're coming back soon,"

As soon as the words left his mouth, the sound of tens of heavily armoured boots filled the corridors outside.

CHAPTER 15

The Praetorian stormed into the chamber.

He had never been in this part of the Fortress.

Although, as he looked around, seeing all the red leather covered books that seem to stretch on for miles. The Praetorian was glad he didn't come here.

He was a man of action, not some nerd that wanted to read books.

He slowed.

He heard voices in the distance.

Because of the endless rows of red books, he had no idea how far away the voices were.

Maybe twenty metres?

He had no idea.

He gripped his Bladed Staff in both hands.

Its thick leather grip felt rough and cold in his armoured hands.

The Praetorian started to walk towards the voices carefully.

Not wanting to make a sound.

An eerie silence surrounded him except the odd whisper from the voices in the distance.

Carefully, looking left, right and behind him. The Praetorian only saw more shelves of books.

Thankfully, the pitch blackness from the stary night sky aided the Praetorian being incredibly hard to see.

Only the odd flicker of yellow candle light went onto him.

The night veiled and wrapped itself around him.

Almost as if it was a signal from the Empress.

She wanted him to succeed.

He shrugged off the ridiculous thought.

The only good thing about this situation could be the fact that he wasn't going to be detected.

Then he cast his mind back to the traitorous guards he had butchered on the way to the Library.

He needed to be quick and effective.

The Praetorian attempted to sniff the air for toxins and other people.

Yet he only got a nose full of foul dusty old musty books.

He hated this place.

Then his mouth turned dry and all he could taste was mustard.

He wanted to leave.

Yet he had a job, no duty to do in the Empress' name.

He was not some mere mortal, he was the Empress' Praetorian and he was above such petty discomforts.

The voices became louder.

He was closer.

The Praetorian dived behind some bookcases.

Peeking over the top of some cold hard books, the Praetorian saw the Lord of Iron pressing his boot into the Chancellor's chest.

He did not care for the Chancellor, but he had to admit he was loyal to the Empress.

He had to do something.

"Chancellor!" he screamed.

After a few moments, the People's Representative and Lord of Iron ran away.

The Praetorian rushed over to the Chancellor and helped him up.

A part of the Praetorian felt pity for this old man then his unconscious memory replayed what the Chancellor declared in the meeting.

He knew the Chancellor could take care of himself.

The Praetorian was about to interrogate the Chancellor when tens of heavy footsteps echoed around the library.

He looked at the Chancellor.

Alvis was unarmed.

The Praetorian doubted he could fight.

Insenguardian soldiers charged in.

Their large metal swords swung in the air.

The Praetorian surged forward.

His Bladed Staff smashed the armour of some.

The Chancellor grabbed a gun from a fallen traitor.

His hands pulsed with pain.

Alvis fired repeatedly.

The Praetorian felt the heat from the bullets on his neck.

The armour of the traitors shattered.

Swinging his Bladed Staff once more, the Praetorian took the initiative.

He smashed the heads of the enemy.

He shattered spines.

Blood spattered all over the walls and floors.

Shards of bone dug into the eyes and faces of the traitors.

Their eyes screamed with pain as blood poured from them.

They begged for death.

The Praetorian provided.

He dived into the combat.

Ripping windpipes from the still living enemy.

He smashed spines over his knees.

The warmth of their blood warmed his armour slightly.

Vapourised blood is all the Praetorian could taste in his mouth.

Shots dented his armour.

Another volley of shots ripped into the Praetorian golden armour.

He spun around.

The bronze and golden warriors of the Covert Military Division stormed the chamber.

They shot at whatever they could.

Their military prowess was impressive.

Whether it be friend or foe. The warriors killed it with a quick cold calculated shot to the head.

The Praetorian grabbed Alvis.

Pulling him behind some bookcases.

The Covert warriors slaughtered everyone in the room.

The Praetorian frowned.

This was not the Will of the Empress.

The Empress made these warriors to end Her enemies.

If he had cared about these soldiers getting slaughtered by their former allies, then he supposed he would be upset.

He looked at the Chancellor.

He noticed the tear in his eyes.

The Praetorian rolled his eyes.

"This is not the time for emotion, Chancellor. We must move,"

The Chancellor did not.

"Come on," the Praetorian firmly urged.

"Fair Son of Insenguard, I am an old man. I will only slow you down. You must go to the cathedral that is where they're based. I will be captured. I will be a man on the inside when they take me. Plus, Fair Son there is a massive force of Gauic soldiers massing nearby. We must be quick. Now go!"

The Praetorian shook his head.

The Covert warriors were coming closer.

"Damn you, old man. The Empress Protects,"

The Praetorian ran away.

He got to the immense cast iron door at the end of the library.

The Praetorian stopped.

He looked to see the Chancellor coming out of

the bookcases.

He didn't even check to see if the Praetorian was here.

Alvis walked head held high towards the enemy.

The Covert warriors looked as if they were going to kill him.

The Representative of the Covert Division marched in wearing his massive bulky bronze and golden armour.

He grabbed the Chancellor.

Pressing a gun firmly in his back.

The Praetorian could only wonder how much pain the old man was in.

Then the Covert Representative marched the Chancellor away.

CHAPTER 16

Kneeling down in the cold dark sewer tunnels under the cathedral, the Praetorian could feel the cold dampness of the ground through his thick golden armour.

Around him, the rest of the Praetorian Guard knelt on the ground as well. Cleaning and checking their swords and guns for the battle ahead.

The cold was stupid down here.

The Praetorian had felt this sort of cold before in the snowy frozen mountains where the Death Cult made their base of operations.

It puzzled the Praetorian how some mere sewer tunnels could be just as cold.

The Praetorian did admire the metre thick walkway on the left-hand side of the sewer tunnel made from bright white marble.

To make matters worse, despite the Praetorian and his brothers in arms having their helmets sealed and the Empress' magical bacteria supplying them with oxygen.

They could all smell the rot and decay that infested these tunnels.

Standing up briefly, the Praetorian looked around.

The moonlight shone brightly through a small metal grid in the ceiling.

When the light hit the rapidly moving water, it dazzled and sparkled. This was only amplified by the shiny smooth marble the tunnel was carved from.

For as far as the Praetorian could see the sewer was a long straight tunnel running under Insenguard with millions if not billions of smaller tunnels growing from this spine.

On the way here, they had lost one member of the Praetorian Guard.

A massive heroic man had fallen into the water whilst climbing up a ladder to get to another tunnel.

Subsequently, the water had drowned him instantly.

Before smashing up his body and armour into

mush.

The Praetorian hated to think what was in this water.

He stared into it.

The top part of this rapidly flowing water was relatively clean.

The bottom part was pitch black with sludge and other unspeakable horrors.

Rats ran across his feet.

He grabbed them.

Ripping their bodies in two.

The Praetorian returned his focus to the surroundings.

Whilst the rushing water was incredibly, almost deafening, this was an advantage.

At least the enemy would be able to hear them coming.

The toxic smells of rot, faecal matter and other dead rats started to intensify.

Even the taste of rotten meat was starting to form on the Praetorian's tongue.

He needed to move.

At least, before the smell became too strong and he along with his men would become unconscious.

This is why he needed the sewer.

This type of operation was reserved for the Covert Division or the Death Cult of Assassins.

Yet neither one of them were in opposition at the moment.

He would love to see the Assassins of the Death Cult right now.

Despite, their jobs being very different.

The Death Cult was probably one of the only Insenguardian fractions, the Praetorian respected for their devotion to the Empress.

With a frown, he banished these thoughts from his mind.

These hopeful thoughts were not going to help him now.

"We move. Remember the plan?" the Praetorian asked with authority.

"Affirmative," they returned.

"We follow the sewer tunnel to the Cathedral

then we burst through and kill the traitors," someone reminded themselves.

The Praetorian nodded.

Leading the way.

As they marched, their feet splashed through puddles of diseased water.

The sound of rapid water drowned it out.

The Praetorian marched ahead.

Jumping over gaps in the tunnel or when the sewer merged with another tunnel.

The light from the grids in the ceiling provided just enough light to see where they were walking.

A scream caught his attention.

He saw a hand sinking into the water.

The Praetorian wanted to dive in and find this person, but it was useless.

No doubt the body would wash up in the next few days.

He looked to the rest of his Praetorian Guard.

Everyone else was okay.

The Praetorian rubbed his forehead.

The more they lost before they reached the cathedral, the more likely the enemy was to win.

Each Praetorian Guard might have been worth a hundred Insenguardian soldiers.

However, with the conspiracy running as deep as it did. The Praetorian was still unsure about victory.

He waved his forces on.

Moments later, they turned a corner.

The Praetorian shot back round.

He indicated three guards were round the corner.

His squad nodded.

Three men crawled up to the corner next to the Praetorian.

They readied their guns.

The Praetorian nodded.

The three Praetorian Guards shot out, found their target and fired.

All three bullets screamed through the air.

They ripped into the flesh of the enemy.

All the bodies fell into the rushing water.

The sound of cracking bone filled the air as the bodies were passed through a barred grid in the water.

For a second, the water turned bright red.

The Praetorian stormed out.

The area was clear.

Walking along the thick marble walkway, the Praetorian looked into the rapidly flowing water.

It was turning more violent and rising.

He didn't know if it was natural or unnatural, but he wanted to leave.

An almighty scream of pain filled the tunnel.

He spun away.

Only to see a Praetorian Guard being turned to fiery red ash as he touched something.

The fiery ash rose up his arm.

Consuming his entire body.

Some Guards rushed to his aid.

The Praetorian waved them back.

Keeping the Guards behind him, the Praetorian looked at the massive sheet of marble in front of him.

It stretched all across the tunnel with the metal grid in the water.

There was a large metal door frame straight in front of the Praetorian. It explained how the enemy got down into the sewer.

Then the Praetorian noticed the glassy reflection of some sort of bubble around the entire marble slab and door.

Rage filled the Praetorian.

He had failed yet again.

He kept failing the Empress.

"What is it, my Lord?"

"I have failed. The enemy must have a witch inside. The entire cathedral is magically shielded. We cannot enter until the shield is gone. The fate of Insenguard now lays in the hands of the Chancellor,"

CHAPTER 17

Alvis was pushed along by Akuma, the Chancellor's body ached from the rough handling and the gun that was being thrusted into his back.

The pain was immense and in some areas the pain pulsed and in other areas the pain radiated with stabbing intensity.

He wanted it all to end.

Yet Alvis knew he would never allow himself to die before the Empress' Work was completed.

The cold metal of the pistol irritated his back.

Akuma in his bronze and gold Knight armour kept pushing Alvis forward.

The Chancellor's feet shuffled along the grey stone floor of the cathedral.

His feet echoed as Alvis tried harder to dig his

feet into the smooth floor.

Akuma kept pushing him.

Alvis felt a bit of confidence within him rise out of nowhere.

Therefore, the Chancellor rose his head and he admired the stunning stone pillars and the structures of previous Emperors, Empresses and other heroic figures from Insenguard's long past that hung on the walls.

It was like the pillars, walls and structures were grown out of the pale white marble. Everything was seamlessly combined.

Alvis even allowed himself to look up at the ceiling of the grand cathedral to admire its breathtaking red and blue stain glass windows as he passed under them.

The moonlight was high in the sky at this point.

Shining bright white light through the stained glass.

Painting everything in a purple light.

However, the purple mixed with the golden light from the candles attached to the walls and everything combined created a calming light that lit the cathedral perfectly.

Looking ahead, Alvis noticed they were leading

him to the Altar. He was too far away from them to see their faces. But he knew some of them were Members of the Council of Insenguard.

Fear gripped him.

There had to be a purpose.

Why not kill him?

Fear gripped Alvis tighter.

Unless they planned to kill him in front of the people.

Unless they were going to make him an example to defiant people.

He needed to escape.

Akuma gripped him tighter.

Knowing what was going through his mind.

The closer Alvis got to the altar, the more his body shivered.

He needed to control himself.

He needed to be ready.

Alvis truly believed that his Empress would help him when the time was right.

If not, he needed to be ready to act. He was not going without a fight.

With a final push, Akuma forced Alvis towards the altar.

It was a grand raised stone platform with an immense marble altar on top.

All the traitors stood in front of it, except the Covert Representative who still jabbed a pistol into his back.

Looking left to right, Alvis grew more and more fearful with every step.

The People's Representative smiled with a long seductive wink at him. She gently stroked her body in her tight black dress.

The Lord Justice flexed at Alvis to show his power and pure raw strength.

Something inside Alvis made him want to stop, but he pushed on.

The Lord of Iron and Emissary stood there staring with murderous intend at the Chancellor.

Alvis felt as if he was a walking slab of meat.

The coldness engulfed him.

Sending immense aching sensation through his joints.

He slowed.

The Covert Representative picked him up.

Through Alvis over his shoulder.

Before, placing him firmly in front of the traitorous members of the Council.

Alvis felt their cold hard gaze burning into him.

Their fury was clear.

"Why bring me here, False Children of Insenguard?" Alvis demanded.

"Oh, Alvis. Oh. It is you who is the False One,"

"I am a loyal son. I am no traitor. Why bring me here?"

"Oh, Chancellor. Oh. Oh, please see reason. We have bought you here to give you a final chance,"

"But only the Covert firth wanted you here," the Lord of Iron added.

Alvis paused.

That was strange.

He thought the People's Representative was in charge, and thus ordered the Chancellor to be here.

Why did Akuma bring him here?

Alvis didn't know.

There would be time for intelligent questions, but he needed the Praetorian to find him first.

"Fair False Daughter, I will never submit to you. Neither will the Empress, she is a God incarnate. Her powers will erase you all when she arrives,"

Hundreds of voices started laughing intensely.

Alvis looked around.

Finally, realising the hundreds if not thousands off traitor soldiers that had filled the cathedral.

There were easily two thousand soldiers here.

Alvis' heart raced.

He was going to die.

"What is so funny, False Children?"

"Oh, Chancellor. Oh, you are so stupid. We have plans for the Empress," Ajanta started.

She waved to a group of troopers to Alvis' far right.

Alvis turned his head.

His face dropped.

His skin buzzed.

A tall extremely thin woman walked towards them.

Her skin was almost transparent, and his long white cloak was ancient.

Alvis looked into the golden eyes of the woman.

He blinked instantly.

Feeling as if he had just stared for minutes at the sun.

Alvis rubbed his eyes.

The woman stopped in front of Alvis.

She nodded her respect to him.

He spat at her.

"My dearest witch, you disgust me. You have…"

Akuma grabbed him.

Dragging him behind the altar.

In front of him, Alvis quickly admired the stunning marble altar.

The blood stains on it concerned him.

Alvis could feel the heat from the cathedral being drained by the altar.

The witch stood three metres in front of Alvis smiling at him.

Akuma stood next to Alvis.

Allowing the Chancellor to smell Akuma's body odour.

He wanted to cough.

He held it in.

The other treacherous members of the Council turned to Alvis.

"Oh, Alvis. Oh, my dear Chancellor. You see we have this mighty witch. A rare dying breed of humans. She will be more than powerful enough to kill the Empress if she does not comply,"

Alvis wanted to lash out and strike.

He wanted nothing more than to jump over this table and rip out the witch's throat.

Yet he knew Akuma would kill him instantly.

As soon as there was a moment, Alvis knew he needed to take it.

However, part of him still wanted to walk away from violence.

He didn't want to take any more lives.

The witch screamed.

The air crackled with magical energy.

"Oh, witch. Oh, what is it?"

The Golden man is here! In the tunnels!

Alvis held his head as the witch smashed her foul words into his mind.

The four Members of the Council stepped towards their forces.

Alvis waited for Akuma to leave.

He stayed.

Akuma whispered gently: "I am surprised, Chancellor that you haven't tried something. Listen carefully. Something is about to happen, and you must act. This entire plan depends on you,"

Alvis paused.

He turned around to look at Akuma.

He was gone.

Only a bronze ribbon laid on the hard-cold stone floor.

Alvis rose an eyebrow.

The witch screamed again.

The cathedral became a hive of activity.

Men and women rushed about.

The Golden Ones are at the shield. They're breaking through.

"For the Empress!" someone screamed.

Alvis thought it was the Praetorian.

He was wrong.

The Bronze warriors of the Covert Division busted out.

Their guns erupted.

Enemies got shattered.

Their blood spattered up the wall.

Their brains painted the floor.

The enemy screamed.

The witch cursed and muttered.

She screamed more.

Alvis knew the Praetorian was doing something.

The odds were not in Akuma's favour.

He had twenty men.

The enemy had thousands.

Alvis thought hard.

Akuma didn't kill him.

He wanted him here.

Alvis looked around.

The witch.

She needed to die.

Alvis was unarmed.

He couldn't charge the witch.

Not at his age.

He looked around.

He noticed the bronze ribbon on the ground.

Alvis knelt down.

The cold stabbed at his joints.

Alvis pulled on the ribbon.

A small hatch opened.

Revealing a pistol.

One shot.

Alvis didn't think.

He grabbed the gun.

Shot up.

He fired.

The bullet screamed through the air.

The witch's head shattered.

Her brain turned to liquid.

Her body slammed onto the ground.

A humming that Alvis hadn't noticed was there, was gone.

The shield had deactivated.

"For the Empress!" Alvis heard the Praetorian scream.

CHAPTER 18

The Praetorian snarled a little as he stared at the glassy magical shield.

Around him, the rest of his golden cladded Guards paced impatiently.

They all wanted their swords and guns to taste traitor blood.

They all wanted to fight and die for the Empress.

Not to protect Insenguard, but to protect Her.

There was something about this entire plot that felt as if its purpose was to kill the Empress.

Rage built inside the Praetorian.

He wanted nothing more than to grab his Bladed Staff and bring it down upon every single living thing nearby.

He banished his dark thoughts.

Instead, he channelled his rage into purpose.

The Praetorian would break this shield and he would kill the traitors.

Breathing in deeply, the Praetorian instantly regretted it as he got a nose full of toxic, diseased filled air.

It smelled horrific.

Turning his head to see his fellow Guards, the Praetorian admired their bright golden armour in the sparkling marble tunnel with the rapidly flowing water next to them.

The moonlight flooded into the tunnel through a metal grid above the flowing water.

Yet the light was dimming.

It was past midnight that was a certainty.

The freezing air of the tunnel was chilling the Praetorian skin.

His body wanted to shiver.

The freezing Roaring water was rising.

It was above his ankle now.

Each second was a fight to stand still against the force of the water.

The water was Roaring loudly as it flowed passed the Praetorian Guard.

He thought one of his Guards sneezed before the water drowned it out.

Slowly, the Praetorian started shivering.

His teeth chattered.

In his rage, the Praetorian grabbed his Bladed Staff.

Rushed over to the glassy shield.

Aimed his swing.

Swung his Bladed Staff.

Another Guard grabbed his arm.

The Praetorian wanted to smash this Guard into mush.

Yet he knew the Guard was right.

If he touched the shield, the Praetorian would die.

He needed to do something.

The water rose to his knee.

The Praetorian was struggling to keep himself upright.

Someone screamed.

A golden warrior fell into the water.

The Praetorian grabbed a golden hand.

It almost caused him to fall.

He let go.

The water turned blood red.

The tunnel was filled with the sound of shattering bones and the wrecking of metal.

He looked at the glassy shield once more.

It showed a perfect golden reflection of himself.

The Praetorian smashed his Bladed Staff into it.

It flashed.

The Praetorian was fine.

No fire engulfed him.

The shield pulsed.

He smashed it again.

It flashed violently.

A distant gunshot went off.

The shield flickered.

"Prepare to move!" the Praetorian ordered.

"Why, my Lord?"

"The Chancellor came through,"

The shield was gone.

The Praetorian charged up the circular stone staircase.

Him and his Praetorian Guard exploded into the cathedral.

The red tainted light shielded them.

They unleashed their storm of bullets and wrath of their swords.

The traitors didn't see them.

Giving the Praetorian Guard time to slaughter them.

The Praetorian slashed and lashed.

The enemy screamed.

Their blood painted the yellow stone walls.

The screams played in perfect symphony.

Their blood warmed up their armour as the Praetorians slaughtered them.

Dark thick pools of red blood painted the grey

stone floor.

The enemy was alerted to the Praetorian Guard now.

Some charged forward.

Some fired their primitive rifles.

A thick stench of gunpowder filled the cathedral.

Followed by a thick cloud of smoke.

The Praetorian smiled.

He saw flashes of rifles from the second floor.

He paused.

His mind confused.

The Praetorian saw the Covert warriors killing their allies.

They could easily kill his warriors.

But they were not.

In fact, the Covert warriors were actively trying to avoid shooting or lashing his warriors.

"Do not engage the Covert warriors for now!" the Praetorian roared, over the noise of the battle.

The Praetorian dived into the thickest part of the battle.

He couldn't see the Chancellor.

He could barely see the altar.

The Praetorian smashed his Bladed Staff into the head of an enemy.

Her face was shattered into shards of bones.

Travelling so fast they killed another soldier.

The Praetorian didn't hesitate.

He kicked up a gun from a dead enemy.

He fired a volley of shots at the traitors.

Their heads exploded.

More gunpowder smoke filled the cathedral.

He needed to find the Chancellor.

His concern grew for the little old man.

Rage filled the Praetorian.

Partially at himself for caring about another besides the Empress.

Partially at the traitors for endangering the Empress.

He didn't care.

The Praetorian punched straight through the

chest of one man.

Another dived onto his back.

The Praetorian ripped him off.

Before, throwing him to the ground and stamping on his head.

It cracked like an egg.

The Praetorian charged forward.

Smashing and lashing the enemy as they came.

His vision was a bloody blur as his helmet was covered in blood.

The Praetorian ripped his helmet off.

Using it to knock the enemy off his feet.

His Guards flanked him.

Whoever the Praetorian knocked down.

His Guards slashed their throats.

Within minutes the Praetorian had cleared half of the cathedral.

Corpses littered the cathedral.

The Covert warriors leapt down from the second floor.

Joining the slaughter.

The Praetorian looked at them.

The Covert warriors nodded.

This was no time to fight these allies.

This was the time to fight for the Empress.

Through the thick grey smoke, more traitors poured out.

The Praetorian became a hurricane of death as he swirled and twirled his Bladed staff in the air.

Shattering armour.

Smashing heads.

Blood and bones spraying everywhere.

Screams filled the cathedral.

More gunshots sounded.

The Praetorian pressed on.

The smoke cleared.

Everyone stopped.

"Keep the entire cathedral. Kill all the traitors," the Praetorian ordered, dismissing everyone.

He looked at the Chancellor.

The Praetorian smiled as he saw the Chancellor saw a smoking gun in front of the altar.

On the floor, the four traitors laid bleeding.

The Praetorian laughed.

How a little old man could overpower these Insenguardians and shoot four Members of the Council, each with extensive military training, was beyond him.

The Praetorian didn't care.

He was... glad to see the Chancellor alive.

He would never voice it, of course.

Yet it was true.

The Praetorian shouted to his men over his shoulder: "Arrest them. I will execute them in a few hours," Then the Praetorian looked at the Chancellor. "You have done well, old man. Now, go. It's two in the morning. Get some rest. All of Insenguard will bear witness to the execution in a few hours,"

CHAPTER 19

Rubbing the sleep away from his eyes, Alvis looked over the massive stone balcony on the edge of the Fortress.

Walking to the edge of the balcony, the Chancellor admired the solid white marble of the balcony and the master-crafted pillars with the golden railing on top.

He loved Insenguard.

Staring out into the distance, Alvis could see the entire empire of Insenguard. All the little houses and all Insenguard's tall dark green forests.

The early morning sun beamed down on the ground causing columns of steam to rise up from the early morning frost.

Even tens of metres high on the balcony, Alvis' breath formed clouds of vapour.

The chilled refreshing air kept him alert.

Alvis' joints might have ached in the cold but he felt at peace.

Perhaps only last week, Alvis would have hated himself for killing once more. He had taken enough lives in Gauic and he was determined not to take anymore.

Alvis had already lost so much to violence. He only wished to end the cycle of blood.

Yet now he knew something.

He was not in the wrong.

Back in Gauic, he had killed to free his people and to allow himself to escape.

Of course, he failed.

He was a failure.

His family died as a result.

Nonetheless, Alvis knew he had to kill the witch and some of those traitors.

At last, he was at peace for his kills and past.

If he didn't kill those people then he and perhaps thousands of others would have died.

Alvis smiled to himself.

Unlike other Gauics, Alvis knew he had lost himself to the bloodlust. He had spared those Members of the Council.

The Chancellor didn't want to.

He wanted to soak his fragile hands in their blood.

But he did not.

A cold gust of wind blew past.

Alvis pulled on his thick black fur coat.

Before, he rubbed his hands together.

The little warmth it generated was enough to keep Alvis happy.

Despite the Chancellor wanting to sleep and recover from the past 24 hours. The Praetorian had commanded everyone in Insenguard was to bear witness to the execution of the traitor Members.

Alvis had heard reports when he first awoke that the bodies of the traitors had been flayed and hacked to pieces. Prior to being spread in the street for all to see what happens to heretics and traitors.

The Chancellor shook his head at the thought.

The hairs on his arms stood up as straight as an arrow.

Breathing in, Alvis could feel the chilled air entering his ancient lungs, and the smelled faint traces of smoke, nature and… Bodies.

Alvis had a half-smile.

He had no doubt the military had a lot of bodies to deal with considering the extent of the conspiracy.

A loud shout caught Alvis' attention.

The Chancellor regally looked down at the crowd fully assembled below the balcony.

Over two million people in their thick black winter coats, huddled together for warmth as they surrounded a large clearing.

All Alvis could see was the massive ring of people followed by the Golden Praetorian Guard keeping back the people, and three pyres inside.

Additionally, there was a golden ant in the middle of the circle with a makeshift table with a person strapped to it.

Alvis knew it was the Praetorian.

He started making a grand speech denouncing these traitors and their conspirators.

Great fear gripped Alvis.

Insenguard's population was twelve million people.

Where were the other ten million?

The Praetorian would have made sure everyone was here to bear witness.

The Chancellor knew the majority of the population had sided with the traitors, and it was only because of the Praetorians' and the loyal military's power did the loyalists overthrow the traitors.

But to think, the Praetorian and Akuma had ten million people killed for treachery.

That was extreme.

Yet that was the Insenguardian way.

Best to purge a cancer before it grows and kills the body.

Alvis had accepted this a while ago, he knew his new country had a dark side.

Equally, he knew the extreme amount of good Insenguard did on the global stage.

A whisper reached him when he got up. Something about the Death Cult of Assassins killing the Gauic government.

Thus, freeing the country to govern itself fairly.

He smiled at the thought of millions of his former countryman being free.

Of course, Alvis could return.

He looked around.

This was his home.

His attention returned to the Praetorian.

Alvis recognised the traitors on the pyres.

The Lord of Iron, Lord Justice and the Emissary were all tied to the pyres.

With a hand gesture, the Praetorian ordered the pyres to be lit.

The traitors screamed in agony as the flames licked their bones.

The flames dancing across their fresh bodies.

Before consuming muscle, flesh, and bone.

Alvis smiled as he heard gasps from the crowd.

The Praetorian shouted another speech.

"This is the price for betraying the Empress. These people were not listening to the Empress. They were manipulating people in the name of a false version of the Empress. And this arch-traitor will pay the ultimate price,"

Alvis lent forward.

He saw Ajanta tied to the make-shift table.

The Praetorian took out a dagger.

Thrusted into her stomach.

Whipped it out.

Rubbed a red paste into the wound.

Then he lit it.

Her body glowed bright red.

She screamed in agony.

Her skins, organs and muscles melted onto the floor.

Within minutes, her body was melted into a boiling hot white paste.

Alvis' heart raced.

Everyone gasped.

Some people screamed in terror.

The Praetorian dismissed them with a wave.

Alvis managed to calm himself.

Then he laughed.

Alvis looked at the sky.

The entire point of this morning was to make examples of these traitors.

The Chancellor could have easily killed these traitors in the cathedral, but he didn't.

For some reason, he just knew that wasn't his purpose.

The Praetorian could have killed all these traitors in secret.

Akuma could have identified the traitor Members and killed them silently.

However, that was never the point.

The battle, the killing, everything needed to be loud.

How else would others be deterred from treachery?

CHAPTER 20

Alvis heard a footstep behind him.

He turned around slowly to see Akuma walk towards him with a mug of coffee in his hand.

Despite, the chilling morning air and the smell of smoke and the taint of burning flesh. The bitterness of the coffee still reached Alvis' nose.

He would love to have some.

Yet Alvis was not going to take anything from Akuma, at risk of death.

The smell of the bitter earthy coffee made the taste of bitter coffee cake form in his mouth.

He would love to chomp down on a piece as the memories of his mother's cooking came flooding back to him.

Looking at Akuma, Alvis admired the man's long

bronze robe made from soft silk, and his white pressed tunic.

Akuma might not have been armed or armoured, but Alvis still felt uneasy.

He wished he was armed.

Akuma walked towards him with confidence, pride and prowess.

The Covert Representative knew he was in control and Alvis was not.

His robe swirled and whirled in the refreshing morning breeze.

Alvis didn't let his eyes leave the Covert Representative.

Alvis pushed himself against the cold marble of the railing on the balcony.

Akuma walked up and leaned on the railing about two metres from Alvis.

Hoping to find a loose piece of marble, the Chancellor let his hand run across the cold marble railing. The smooth marble gently rubbing against his fingers.

He couldn't find any loose pieces.

Akuma stood there.

Staring out into the distance. Admiring Insenguard's natural beauty.

Alvis wanted to appear relaxed.

He turned around and joined Akuma looking out at Insenguard's lush green forests.

The smell of burning bodies and bitter coffee still filled the air.

The wind picked up.

Howling pass Alvis' ears.

The freezing wind felt like sandpaper against his face.

His joints pulsed with pain from the cold.

He needed to get inside.

However, another part of him wanted to find out why Akuma was here.

The Covert Representative turned to face him.

Alvis' heart raced.

Sweat started to form on his forehead.

It turned to ice quickly.

Akuma had a deep short snort.

"Dear Akuma, why do you come to grace me with your presence?"

"Come, come now, Chancellor. You do not need to be polite with me. You have questions. The Praetorian certainly did. Ask them,"

Alvis wasn't going to miss his chance.

"Dearest Akuma, why?"

"Ha, why, what? Why I didn't turn traitor? Why I pretended?"

Alvis nodded.

"The answer is simple. Insenguard is the most powerful country on the planet. Some consider me extreme and I agree. Insenguard will rise up one day. The Empress will see the world for what it is,"

"What is that, dear child?"

"Corrupt. Humanity, dwarfs, all species are corrupted and cannot be left to their own devices. Insenguard already intervenes when required to free people. We should rule the people. Everyone will be free and be able to enjoy life. It is only a matter of time before the Empress or the Ruler after Her realises this,"

Alvis was wide eyed.

He didn't like what he was hearing.

However, he was here, and he was hearing it.

"So, to answer your question, Lord Chancellor. If the traitors won, Insenguard would have fallen into the hands of darker powers. The best way to bring about my wishes- is to make sure the Empress stays in power. Then I will guide Insenguard to my realisation,"

It horrified Alvis.

This must be treachery.

Insenguard was no tyrannical country.

It was a country of peace and freedom.

In that moment, Alvis vowed to himself to stop Akuma whatever the cost.

Then it hit him.

The Empress had given him a purpose all along.

His purpose was to protect Insenguard from the ambitions of others, and that is what he fully intended to do.

Akuma started to walk away.

"Dear Akuma, the traitors are dead. So, is everything over and everything is a success?"

"Of course, my Lord Chancellor. Just as the Empress willed it,"

Author's Note

Thank you for reading this book.

I really hope you enjoyed the story.

Personally, I loved writing the book because in this story I wanted to focus on characters.

This is why I created a range of hopefully enjoyable characters. Like, the posh and formal Chancellor Alvis, the flexing, womanising Lord Justice, and the seductive People's Representative.

I thought the People's Representative was hilarious to write because of her dialogue.

Hopefully, you laughed too!

The inspiration for the book came from one of my favourite books of all: The Regent's Shadow by Chris Wright.

I got to the end of the book and I loved it so much that I wanted to use it to inspire one of my own books.

Also, in case you've read the rest of the books in the series: Winter's Coming, Winter's Hunt and Winter's Revenge. In this book, I wanted to write about what happens when the Empress leaves Insenguard to pursuit the Cult.

Personally, I loved this book, but it was very different to what I usually write. Since I typically write world or even galaxy expanding stories.

Therefore, this story set in one country and a small country at that- was very domestic for me.

However, I still loved it, the plot and the characters.

Finally, I just wanted to thank you for reading the book and I really hope you enjoyed it!

Thank you for reading. If you liked this book please consider leaving an honest review and if you want more then please check out the link below to get your FREE and EXCLUSIVE short story.

GET YOUR FREE EXCLUSIVE WINTER SHORT STORY HERE!

https://www.subscribepage.com/wintersignup

Thank you for reading.

I hoped you enjoyed it.

If you want a FREE book and keep up to date about new books and project. Then please sign up for my newsletter at www.connorwhiteley.net/

Have a great day.

About the author:

Connor Whiteley is the author of over 20 books in the sci-fi fantasy, nonfiction psychology and books for writer's genre and he is a Human Branding Speaker and Consultant.

He is a passionate Warhammer 40,000 reader, psychology student and author.

Who narrates his own audiobooks and he hosts The Psychology World Podcast.

All whilst studying Psychology at the University of Kent, England.

Also, he was a former Explorer Scout where he gave a speech to the Maltese President in August 2018 and he attended Prince Charles' 70th Birthday Party at Buckingham Palace in May 2018.

Plus, he is a self-confessed coffee lover!

Please follow me on:

Website: www.connorwhiteley.net

Twitter: @scifiwhiteley

Please leave on honest review as this helps with the discoverability of the book and I truly appreciate it.

Thank you for reading. I hope you've enjoyed.

WINTER'S DISSENSION

All books in 'An Introductory Series':

BIOLOGICAL PSYCHOLOGY 2ND EDITION

COGNITIVE PSYCHOLOGY 2ND EDITION

SOCIOCULTURAL PSYCHOLOGY- 2ND EDITION

ABNORMAL PSYCHOLOGY 2ND EDITION

PSYCHOLOGY OF HUMAN RELATIONSHIPS- 2ND EDITION

DEVELOPMENTAL PSYCHOLOGY 2ND EDITION

HEALTH PSYCHOLOGY

RESEARCH IN PSYCHOLOGY

A GUIDE TO MENTAL HEALTH AND TREATMENT AROUND THE WORLD- A GLOBAL LOOK AT DEPRESSION

FORENSIC PSYCHOLOGY

CLINICAL PSYCHOLOGY

CONNOR WHITELEY

FORMULATION IN PSYCHOTHERAPY

Other books by Connor Whiteley:

THE ANGEL OF RETURN

THE ANGEL OF FREEDOM

GARRO: GALAXY'S END

GARRO: RISE OF THE ORDER

GARRO: END TIMES

GARRO: SHORT STORIES

GARRO: COLLECTION

GARRO: HERESY

GARRO: FAITHLESS

GARRO: DESTROYER OF WORLDS

GARRO: COLLECTIONS BOOK 4-6

GARRO: MISTRESS OF BLOOD

GARRO: BEACON OF HOPE

GARRO: END OF DAYS

WINTER'S COMING

WINTER'S HUNT

CONNOR WHITELEY

WINTER'S REVENGE

WINTER'S DISSENSION

Companion guides:

BIOLOGICAL PSYCHOLOGY 2ND EDITION WORKBOOK

COGNITIVE PSYCHOLOGY 2ND EDITION WORKBOOK

SOCIOCULTURAL PSYCHOLOGY 2ND EDITION WORKBOOK

ABNORMAL PSYCHOLOGY 2ND EDITION WORKBOOK

PSYCHOLOGY OF HUMAN RELATIONSHIPS 2ND EDITION WORKBOOK

HEALTH PSYCHOLOGY WORKBOOK

FORENSIC PSYCHOLOGY WORKBOOK

Audiobooks by Connor Whiteley:

BIOLOGICAL PSYCHOLOGY

COGNITIVE PSYCHOLOGY

SOCIOCULTURAL PSYCHOLOGY

ABNORMAL PSYCHOLOGY

PSYCHOLOGY OF HUMAN RELATIONSHIPS

HEALTH PSYCHOLOGY

DEVELOPMENTAL PSYCHOLOGY

RESEARCH IN PSYCHOLOGY

FORENSIC PSYCHOLOGY

GARRO: GALAXY'S END

GARRO: RISE OF THE ORDER

GARRO: SHORT STORIES

GARRO: END TIMES

GARRO: COLLECTION

GARRO: HERESY

[GARRO: FAITHLESS](#)

[GARRO: DESTROYER OF WORLDS](#)

[GARRO: COLLECTION BOOKS 4-6](#)

[GARRO: COLLECTION BOOKS 1-6](#)

Business books:

[TIME MANAGEMENT: A GUIDE FOR STUDENTS AND WORKERS](#)

[LEADERSHIP: WHAT MAKES A GOOD LEADER? A GUIDE FOR STUDENTS AND WORKERS.](#)

[BUSINESS SKILLS: HOW TO SURVIVE THE BUSINESS WORLD? A GUIDE FOR STUDENTS, EMPLOYEES AND EMPLOYERS.](#)

[BUSINESS COLLECTION](#)

GET YOUR FREE BOOK AT:
[WWW.CONNORWHITELEY.NET](#)

www.ingramcontent.com/pod-product-compliance
Lightning Source LLC
LaVergne TN
LVHW012044070526
838202LV00056B/5592